ARKHAM HORROR

It is the height of the Roaring Twenties – a fresh enthusiasm for the arts, science, and exploration of the past have opened doors to a wider world, and beyond...

And yet, a dark shadow grows over the town of Arkham. Alien entities known as Ancient Ones lurk in the emptiness beyond space and time, writhing at the thresholds between worlds.

Occult rituals must be stopped and alien creatures destroyed before the Ancient Ones make our world their ruined dominion.

Only a handful of brave souls with inquisitive minds and the will to act stand against the horrors threatening to tear this world apart.

Will they prevail?

T0190638

ALSO AVAILABLE IN ARKHAM HORROR

THE
DARKNESS
OVER
ARKHAM

JONATHAN GREEN

ACONYTE

First published by Aconyte Books in 2024

ISBN 978 1 83908 295 5

Ebook ISBN 978 1 83908 296 2

Technical assistance by Victor Cheng

Cover art by Joshua Cairós • Book design by Nick Tyler

Interior art by Cristi Balanescu, Joshua Cairós, Matthew Cowdery, Richard Jossy, Alexander Karcz, Robert Laskey, Stephen Somers & Magali Villeneuve

Distributed in North America by Simon & Schuster Inc, New York, USA

Printed in the United States of America

9 8 7 6 5 4 3 2 1

ACONYTE BOOKS

An imprint of Asmodee Entertainment Ltd

Mercury House, Shipstones Business Centre

North Gate, Nottingham NG7 7FN, UK

aconytebooks.com // twitter.com/aconytebooks

For Jake.

GREETINGS, INVESTIGATOR.

Welcome to Arkham.

By entering the pages of this Investigators Gamebook, you have taken on the role of one of the brave Investigators driven to uncover the truth behind the strange goings-on in the legend haunted city of Arkham.

A gamebook is both a book and a game. The choices you make – as well as your success in tests of **WILLPOWER**, **INTELLECT** and **COMBAT** – will determine the route you travel through the book, deciding victory or defeat in your attempts to unravel the sinister mystery within. If you've played other adventure gamebooks, you'll be familiar with the concept, but this is Arkham and a few things are a little… different. So, you'll want to read over the next couple of pages before your investigation begins.

Unlike most other kinds of games, you don't need to learn all the rules before you start to play, but you should embrace what it means to be an Investigator to the fullest. Take note of names, locations, and anything else that might prove advantageous to you on your adventure. Some clues are obvious while others are obscure. If you're new to this type of adventure, or simply eager to begin, you have the choice to bypass some of the following instructions and leap right in. The book presents the choices you will be required to make and the tests that you will face as you go along. However, if you're curious to understand the further complexities, there are just a few things you will need before you start, and additional pointers it will prove useful to know.

WHAT YOU WILL NEED

You will need some ordinary six-sided dice – a couple is plenty. Grab them now…. good work. You will also need something to keep track of your Investigator's progress. You can use (and photocopy, if you wish) the character sheet on page 283, or a notepad or piece of paper. You can also download character sheets from our website at *https://aconytebooks.com/investigators*. You'll need something to write with, and as your Investigator can both acquire and lose CLUES, RESOURCES, HEALTH, SANITY, [ITEMS], and {ABILITIES} over the course of their investigation, a pencil is ideal. Most importantly, you'll need to choose the Investigator whose role you will be playing once you begin the adventure.

CHOOSING AN INVESTIGATOR

You can find Investigator profiles for three Investigators on pages **13**, **14**, and **15**: the waitress Agnes Baker, the boxer Nathaniel Cho, and the reporter Rex Murphy. There are more Investigators you'll find as downloads on our website, but if this is your first time playing through an Investigators Gamebook, we recommend using one of the three Investigators that come with this book first.

Each Investigator's profile shows all their skills, abilities, weaknesses, and items, as well as their starting HEALTH and SANITY. Before you begin, you should copy these over to your character sheet – or simply download the pre-filled version of the character sheet for your chosen Investigator from our website.

CHARACTER SHEETS

Now that you have your character sheet, you are about ready to begin, but first it's useful to know a little more about the information your character sheet presents. Your character sheet represents you, in the role of your chosen Investigator. You are them now, and their fate is your fate. The character sheet tracks your progress through a number of game stats, and also provides space to record anything you pick up along the way, such as CLUES and RESOURCES.

SKILLS: WILLPOWER, INTELLECT AND COMBAT

Each investigator has three skills: WILLPOWER, INTELLECT and COMBAT. Throughout the adventure, you'll face challenges which test these skills in a variety of different ways. When facing one of these tests, the entry in question will explain how to resolve it. Skills are represented by a number, and this number may occasionally change during the investigation.

HEALTH AND SANITY

These two game stats describe your Investigator's current physical and mental wellbeing. Like skills, they are represented by a number, and tend to go down as the adventure goes on – in fact, they can even go negative – although they can also go up. A lower HEALTH or SANITY score will negatively impact your chances when faced with various challenges. Once these stats dip below zero, however, things will be continuously affected, and we urge you to reference your character sheet to account for those impacts. Try not to lose your mind, if you please.

ABILITIES AND WEAKNESSES

Abilities and Weaknesses represent special aptitudes or limitations peculiar to your chosen Investigator. Most Investigators start with a small number of each, and you may acquire other types of Abilities and Weaknesses as your investigation progresses. These Abilities and Weaknesses are represented by keywords, which don't do anything in and of themselves, but which may trigger bonuses or penalties, or other effects, depending on the challenges you encounter during the adventure. You don't need to memorize your Investigator's Abilities and Weaknesses. Instead, when an entry mentions an Ability or Weakness, you should check on your character sheet to see whether or not the effects described apply to you.

Sometimes, however, you may gain an Ability or Weakness as your investigation progresses. The mysteries surrounding Arkham are not for the faint of heart and can rattle any hardened Investigator, gifting you with proclivities such as {HAUNTED} or {PARANOIA} that don't simply fade away. Yet, great powers and abilities can also be obtained… if one has the fortitude and cleverness to earn them. These too, for good or for ill, do not simply disappear.

Most Investigators also start with a Major Ability and a Major Weakness. You can only ever have one of each of these, and you can't lose or gain them during the course of an adventure. These Major Abilities and Major Weaknesses represent key aspects of your Investigator's personality, and each gives you a special rule, which make playing the adventure unique to you and your character. They are detailed on your Investigator profile.

DOOM

The deepening mysteries and their consequences impact not just you, but the world around you. As Arkham strains against the darkness plotting to envelop it, the state of the environment shifts accordingly. DOOM will appear as you further unravel the mystery contained within, representing a worsening state for humanity, but a more favorable one for the creatures and Ancient Ones influencing Arkham. Obtaining DOOM is most unadvisable. Try not to hand the universe over to the eldritch beings, won't you?

ITEMS

Items are exactly what you would expect – various objects your Investigator might carry with them or pick up along the way. For example, right now you have your [PENCIL] and your [SIX-SIDED DICE]. These items are keywords without any special properties, but which may prove useful in certain situations over the course of the adventure.

Most Investigators possess one starting item, representing an especially useful or cherished personal possession that can be found on their Investigator profile, which also provides you with a special rule that may prove useful at points in the adventure. These items are specific to that particular Investigator and cannot be lost, transferred, or gained.

As mentioned, other objects can be found and collected during your investigation as you journey through Arkham and speak with its eccentric inhabitants, but you might stumble across other items on your journey that, unless they are notated in square brackets like your [PENCIL], alas, cannot be picked up. Record items that you can pick up on your Character Sheet but select with caution. Some items may

be used to fight horrific creatures, while others might crumble the sanity you hold dear. Power corrupts, or so we're told...

CLUES AND RESOURCES

As an Investigator, you are hopefully going to uncover lots of CLUES along the way, as well as picking up RESOURCES that can help you out when things get tough. Investigators begin with 0 CLUES and 0 RESOURCES but can acquire them over the course of the adventure. When you acquire a CLUE or RESOURCES, add a tally mark to the relevant box on your Character Sheet. There will be times when you have the opportunity to spend a CLUE or RESOURCES to make some of the tests or puzzles you face a little easier. If you choose to do so, strike out the appropriate number of tally marks on your Character Sheet, or reference your Investigator profile for Investigator-specific abilities regarding spending CLUES and RESOURCES.

READY TO BEGIN?

We certainly hope so. This is not going to be easy but finding the courage to begin is the hardest part. From here on, your chances are going to be decided by the choices you make and the path you choose to follow – not to mention skill and a little luck.

This gamebook consists of individual numbered entries. Based on your choices – or your success in various test, challenges, and puzzles – you'll be instructed to move to a specific numbered entry at the end of each step. If you're ready to begin, turn the page, read the prologue for your chosen Investigator, and good luck. Arkham, and the world as we know it, is in your hands.

Agnes Baker's Investigator Profile

Agnes Baker

THE WAITRESS

5	**2**	**2**	**6**	**8**
WILLPOWER	INTELLECT	COMBAT	HEALTH	SANITY

STARTING ITEM

[HEIRLOOM OF HYPERBOREA]:
If you succeed in a test using your **WILLPOWER**, gain +**1 RESOURCE**.

MAJOR ABILITY

{SORCERER}

Once per adventure, you may use your **WILLPOWER** instead of your **COMBAT** in a fight or test.

MAJOR WEAKNESS

{DARK MEMORIES}

Each time you spend a **CLUE**, roll a dice. On a roll of a 1, Agnes loses -**1 SANITY**.

OTHER ABILITIES

{MYSTIC}
{SORCERY}
{ARCANE STUDIES}

OTHER WEAKNESSES

{HAUNTED}

Nathaniel Cho's Investigator Profile

Nathaniel Cho

THE BOXER

 3 WILLPOWER   **2** INTELLECT   **5** COMBAT   **9** HEALTH   **6** SANITY

STARTING ITEM

[HIDDEN WEAPON]:
Once per adventure,
you may add +3 to your COMBAT.

MAJOR ABILITY

{BOXER}

If you roll a 6 while using your COMBAT, add +1 to your total score. (If you are rolling more than one dice, add +1 for each 6. you roll.)

OTHER ABILITIES

{GUARDIAN}
{FIGHTER}
{TOUGH}

MAJOR WEAKNESS

{HUNTED BY THE MOB}

Each time you gain a RESOURCE, roll a die. If the score is below your current number of RESOURCE, do not gain a RESOURCE.

OTHER WEAKNESSES

{CRIMINAL}

Rex Murphy's Investigator Profile

Rex Murphy
THE REPORTER

3 WILLPOWER

4 INTELLECT

2 COMBAT

6 HEALTH

9 SANITY

STARTING ITEM

[REPORTER'S NOTEBOOK]:
You begin with +1 CLUE.

MAJOR ABILITY
{REPORTER}

If you roll a 6 while using your INTELLECT, gain +1 CLUE.

MAJOR WEAKNESS
{REX'S CURSE}

If you roll a double when using your INTELLECT or WILLPOWER, treat the score on each dice as a 1.

OTHER ABILITIES
{SEEKER}

OTHER WEAKNESSES
{CURSED}

AGNES

It's the end of another long, hard shift at the diner, but working as a waitress at Velma's remains the perfect cover for you. It means you can pursue any threads that might provide you with more information about your past life as a powerful sorcerer and allows you to continue the battle your former self started, fighting the machinations of the myriad eldritch powers that would see Arkham destroyed.

Some of the diner's clientele would probably be shocked to learn that the town's history of witchcraft and strange goings-on was the reason you moved to Arkham. Some, but not all. Velma's is a hotbed for gossip and rumor relating to Arkham's dark underbelly, and your nightmares concerning black-robed figures intoning chilling incantations have only worsened in recent days.

Now turn to **1**.

NATHANIEL

It has been some time since you turned your back on the boxing ring, after the O'Bannion gang pressed you into fixing fights for their own financial reward. That wasn't how you had envisioned your boxing career going, but if that was how it had to be, you wanted no part of it. And so, you quit and now put your fists to good use protecting the innocent citizens of Arkham from the mob.

Tonight, you intend to patrol the streets as usual. There is something brewing; you can feel it in the air, like the change in pressure before a storm. But before setting out on patrol, you stop in at Velma's Diner to fortify yourself with a coffee and a slice of cherry pie, in readiness for whatever might lie ahead.

Now turn to **1**.

REX

The lead to another story lost, this time because the astrophysicist appears to have upped and gone. Certainly no one at the Warren Observatory seemed to know where Dr Waugh was when you questioned them earlier this afternoon. You're lucky that Doyle Jeffries, editor of the *Arkham Advertiser*, seems to like you, otherwise you're not sure how much longer you could last in this town.

You stare at the swirling mud-black liquid as you stir your coffee. Then, when you're sure none of the diner's staff are looking, you take out the bottle of [**WHISKEY**] and quickly pour some into the cup before returning the bottle to your coat pocket.

As you sip the boosted beverage, you console yourself with the fact that Velma's Diner is somewhere that even the most rookie reporter could sniff out a story. And so, you wait.

Now turn to **1**.

1

Velma's Diner is a popular hangout in the town of Arkham. It provides precisely what its clientele expects of a diner: hot coffee, hearty home-cooked food, and a place to rest out of the wind and rain. But it's not the kind of place you can stay forever. Through the windows, in the world beyond the diner, you can see the sun creeping toward the fir-lined hills to the west of Arkham. It's time for you to leave.

You begin gathering your things, when a raised voice take hold of your attention and your eyes lock on one of the booths where two older people are sitting. One is a gray bearded man, while the other is a thin, spiky woman, her silvery hair cut into a severe bob. Their clothes are not only befitting of their advancing years but also suggest that they are of an academic persuasion. You know the type well. There are plenty to be found in Arkham.

As if aware that their heated exchange has drawn your gaze, the woman gives you a caustic stare before lowering her voice and resuming her intent discussion with the man. You may not be able to hear what she is saying, but from her body language – the way she leans forward, her shoulders hunched, one index finger stabbing at the air – it is clear that she is unhappy about something. The man, on the other hand, has assumed an aloof attitude toward their exchange and seems to say barely anything in response to the woman's tirade.

Between them are two empty mugs and a plate smeared with grease. The uncleared crockery is attracting flies that always seem to manage to sneak into the diner through the open doors and windows. However, their presence seems unusual at this time of year. One scuttles about the table, no doubt dining on the scattered sugar crystals that dust the melamine surface. As you watch, you become hypnotized by its unpredictable jittering dance and are startled when the woman slams her hand down on top of it in a moment of impassioned anger.

As the man mutters something back at her, she pulls her hand back and, in the blink of an eye, puts her fingers to her lips as if passing something to her mouth. The action happens so quickly you wonder if it was all in your imagination. But when you glance back at the table, the fly has gone.

You feel a strange twist in your stomach. You have been exposed to unexplainable, strange behavior before and it never ends well. No matter how peculiar the town of Arkham is, it is still your home, and you feel compelled to protect it no matter what. But did you really witness the old woman eat a fly?

Your ruminations on what you did or did not see are the matter of a fleeting second as the woman abruptly stands. Clearly, whatever the old man said has drawn things to a conclusion. She storms out of the diner. Mere moments later, having deposited a crumpled dollar bill on the table, the man follows, but you do not get the impression that the woman will have waited for him.

It is only after the couple have left, and the diner door has swung shut behind the man that you notice a notebook lying on the floor next to the booth where the pair were sitting. It is nothing like the notepads used by those who wait tables at the diner to take customers' orders, so you can only assume one of the academics must have dropped it.

Without drawing attention to yourself, you approach

the table and, crouching down, pick up [DR BLAINE'S NOTEBOOK]. Flicking through it, you see that the pages are filled with handwritten notes in a language you don't understand.

> If you want to take a moment to study the jotter more carefully, turn to **45**.
>
> If you want to leave the diner in pursuit of the academics and return the notebook to its rightful owner, turn to **75**.

Oh dear, it looks like you've visited somewhere you shouldn't have. And you should be careful when it comes to entering unknown places in the town of Arkham, Massachusetts.

If you're reading this because you finished the first section and simply kept on going, we must warn you that you are going to get confused, not to mention lost, very quickly, and that way madness lies. This book really only makes sense if you hop from entry to entry, according to the choices you make and the directions you're given. We suggest you go back and decide what you want to do regarding the dropped notebook.

Then again, maybe you're here because you think this section is the solution to one of the puzzles in the book. Sorry, wrong again. Whoever said that finding all those Easter Eggs was going to be easy? But award yourself a Secret anyway. Take the SECRET: *Lost in Arkham*.

But perhaps you're here because you are actively looking for Secrets. Fair enough, here's one on us. Take the SECRET: *Secrets of the Ancient Ones.*

> Now go back to whatever it was you were doing before, which might well mean going back to **1**.

3

It appears that you have run into a dead end. Without any idea where to go in search of further clues, the mystery of Dr Blaine's fate will remain just that – a mystery.

You do not know what is going on or if any of what you have discovered signifies, but you feel on edge, as if something terrible threatens Arkham. From this day on, you will go about your life with one eye always looking over your shoulder because you know, deep in your bones, that a great darkness is gathering over Arkham, and none shall escape its pall.

Take the SECRET: *Dark Omens.*
The End.

4

You call out to the nurse, asking if she can help you. She hesitates before turning and walking back down the passageway toward you. "What can I do for you?" she asks. Rather than sounding like a genuine offer of aid, it comes across as if the nurse is suspicious of you.

"I was wondering if Dr Blaine has been brought in yet," you tell her, deciding you have nothing to lose by telling the truth, considering you are already waiting outside the morgue.

"I believe so," the woman says. "He'll be in there." She indicates the door behind you with a nod.

"Thank you…?" You peer at her badge but can't read it properly

She hesitates before answering, " Ruth Turner."

"You've been most helpful, Ms Turner."

"You're welcome. Now if you will excuse me…"

She returns to her gurney, on which lies a body covered by a sheet, and continues on her way. She passes around a corner and is gone.

Take the SECRET: *The Mortician*.

It is only then that you notice the [TOE-TAG] lying on the floor. Picking it up you see that the name on it reads "John Doe." You wonder if the tag fell off the body on the gurney and briefly consider going after Nurse Turner to ask, before thinking better of it.

> Add the [TOE-TAG] to your Character Sheet, if you wish, and turn to **36**.

While you are talking to the policeman, the two cops emerge from the building again and beckon the sergeant and his rookie colleague over. Words are exchanged and orders are issued. You hazard to ask the sergeant what has happened.

"I'm sorry to say that a body has been found in a third story office, and that this has now become a homicide investigation," the sergeant says, gruffly.

So, it is as you feared. Dr Blaine, the owner of the notebook, which is still in your pocket, was murdered by that monster you battled. Shivering, you consider yourself lucky to have escaped with your life.

Thinking of the jotter, you wonder if that was why the aging academic was killed. You had better be wary about who learns that [DR BLAINE'S NOTEBOOK] is in your possession, since you could be in terrible danger yourself. But you still have no idea what is actually written in Dr Blaine's jotter and can't help thinking that the key to solving this mystery lies within.

> If you want to make your way to Ye Olde Magick Shoppe in Uptown in the hope of finding someone who can help you decode Dr Blaine's cryptic jottings, turn to **171**.
>
> If you want to watch how the situation develops here at Miskatonic University, but at a distance, turn to **41**.

6

You consider the words of the prophecy once more. You're not certain what "when the moon in darkness dies" means, but it sounds ominous. And "then a new god shall arise" sounds even worse. Combined with "one from three shall claim the prize" makes you wonder if there are three factions working to bring the prophecy about... and what that could mean for Arkham.

Take the SECRET: *Hidden Four.*

Could Dr Blaine have been involved with one of those factions? And if he was, does that mean this Professor Nidus is as well? Perhaps that was what they were arguing about. But he also had his doubts about Dr Waugh the astrophysicist. What part does he have to play in all this?

Considering Dr Blaine is out of the picture, if you are going to get to the bottom of what actually happened to him, you are going to need to investigate his rivals: Professor Nidus and Dr Waugh. But which of them do you want to look into first?

If you want to look into Professor Nidus, turn to **125.**
If you want to find out more about Dr Waugh, turn to **155.**

7

Taking a closer look at the list of dates, and a book that is open at a page covered with charts relating to the orbit of the moon, it becomes clear that whoever these papers belong to – is it Dr Waugh? – has calculated that an eclipse of the moon will occur this very night.

> Take **+1 CLUE** and turn to **170**.

8

You rattle the door even harder, your eyes fixed on the slight gap between them, and see what looks like a piece of wood – circular in cross-section and an inch in diameter. It looks like someone has barred the door by threading the pole of a broom or mop through the handle and a hook on the wall on the other side.

You look left and right, desperately scouring your surroundings for anything you could use to shift the pole.

> If you have a [**BONESAW**], turn to **295**.
> If not, turn to **270**.

9

You are so lost in thought that it takes a moment for you to register what your subconscious hears loud and clear. When you do, you slam the book shut in shock. You can hear a sound like the chirruping of crickets and the clicking of cicadas. Worse than that, it is coming from inside one of the display cases mounted on the wall behind you.

Disbelief outweighing your fear, you cross the room at a snail's pace, your eyes fixed on a large rose chafer beetle, its carapace the color of engine oil in a puddle of rainwater. Its outstretched wings tremble and then are still. A heartbeat later, the same thing happens again. Out of the corner of your eye, you see an emerald bottle fly in another of the specimen cases do the same thing. Your breathing quickens.

Turning your attention from the beetle to the fly, you watch as its legs twitch in a frustrated spasming dance, and its wings start to flicker. It is as if the fly is trying to free itself from the steel pin that runs right through its body, securing it to the board beneath.

Fascination turns to horror as fear overwhelms your disbelief and the implications of what you are witnessing begin to assert themselves.

Make a panic test. Roll one die and add your **WILLPOWER**. You may spend **1 RESOURCES** to roll two dice and pick the highest. If you have the Weakness {HAUNTED}, deduct 1. What's the result?

> Total of 9 or more: turn to **43**.
> 8 or less: turn to **22**.

Warily, you approach the body. The man doesn't move, and you feel an icy sensation creep down your spine. Is he dead? His eyes are closed, and you cannot see any obvious signs that he is breathing. However, neither can you see any obvious signs of injury. You know there are some conditions that can give the appearance of death while the person remains alive. Perhaps this is the case here. You hope so.

Steeling yourself, you reach a hand toward his exposed throat and press the tips of your fingers against his neck. The skin feels cold and clammy. You cannot make out a pulse. Suddenly the window bangs again in the wind, making you start, and you snatch your hand away.

You doubt there's anything you can do for the man now, but perhaps you could get help, in case there is even the slimmest chance that he is still alive.

If you want to get help, turn to **28**.
If you want to go over to the open window, turn to **52**.

The flickering streetlamps guide you to a large house on the scale of a colonial mansion, but one that is a vision of crumbling grandeur. Abaddan House – as a plaque reads at the entrance – must have been glorious once, but now it is quite apparent that it is falling into disrepair. It is a curious mix of the palatial and the gothic, with a pillared colonnade at the front but the pointed mullioned windows of a German castle. Take the SECRET: *Location Nine*.

It stands apart from the other properties in this neighborhood on a large plot of land and is screened from the road by a thick yew hedge. A light in the porch shines above the front door and you approach the house along a wide gravel drive. There is no one about, and the grounds are eerily quiet, but you can't shake the feeling that there are eyes on you as you make your way toward the mansion.

> If you want to approach the front door, turn to **18**.
> If you want to leave the drive and use the deeper darkness pooling between the trees to creep around the side of the house, turn to **120**.

When you lay the blueprint over your copy of the gardener's plan, and shine a light behind it, you see that a tunnel that ostensibly leads to an icehouse also connects to a wine cellar under the house. Take the SECRET: *Hidden Seven.*

"It has to be worth a try if it means we can make our way into the house unseen by any members of the cult or their servants," says Dr Blaine.

You're not sure what he means by "servants" in this context, but you can't shift the feeling that he's not talking about footmen or housemaids.

And so, the two of you set off across the overgrown lawns behind the house and into the scrubby orchard, wherein lies the brick-lined entrance to the icehouse tunnel. The tunnel is only wide enough for you to walk in single file, and you stoop to avoid hitting your head on the damp brick roof. If you have the Weakness {CLAUSTROPHOBIA}, lose -1 WILLPOWER.

As you proceed along the dank passage, Dr Blaine shining a light from behind you, you find yourselves effectively retracing your steps across the grounds but now ten feet beneath them. Halfway to the house you reach the conical icehouse itself. Just as you suspected, the passageway continues toward the house, but your way is barred by a rusted iron gate.

Fortunately, the gate is closed but not locked and opens with a loud creak when you give it a shove. However, before you can go any further, Dr Blaine puts a hand to your shoulder causing you to pause.

"Wait," comes the doctor's voice. "You must sever the eldritch barrier that protects this place, as well as breach any physical obstructions. Take out the blade." You hesitate before doing as he says. "Like this," he says, reaching around and taking hold of your wrist and directing you to make slashing motions with the scalloped cutting edge. When he is done, he releases your wrist and lets your arm drop. "We may now proceed," he says with what sounds like a sigh of released tension.

An icy sensation trickles down your spine. What kind of promises can he have made that mean he can be kept from stepping within the bounds of the property unless the mystical wards protecting it are banished first?

But you are committed to this course of action now and so continue along the tunnel, certain that you have more to fear from what lies within the house than you do from Dr Blaine. The tunnel leads to a flight of steps that you climb to a trapdoor. This opens easily and you find yourselves in the wine cellar demarcated on the plan of the house. From the cellar you pass through an undecorated wooden door into a pantry. All manner of foodstuffs surround you.

> If you want to take a closer look at what is to be found within the pantry, turn to **35**.
> If you would prefer to press on without any delay, turn to **54**.

A scream suddenly rises from the woman standing atop the stone platform, a scream that embodies all the high priestess's rage and frustration and, for the first time, the Cult of Assimilation falters in its chanting. All eyes follow her gaze, including yours.

Beyond the glass panels that form the roof of the conservatory, the night sky is clear of clouds. You can see the round white orb of the moon, set amid a myriad of diamond stars. But at the same time, you can see the Earth's shadow is starting to slowly creep across the face of the moon.

But what is the significance of this to cause such a reaction in Professor Nidus? Did her ritual need to be completed before the eclipse occurred? In the next moment, you have your answer. There is something approaching Abaddan House through the night, and as it draws closer, the light filling the conservatory bathes the hideous, impossible monstrosity in a jaundice-yellow glow.

You have seen too many unbelievable things this night, but nothing like what approaches the Cult of Assimilation's stronghold now. In the most basic sense, it looks like a bird, in that it has outstretched wings and a beak-like mouth. But in truth its wings are colossal, like those of some giant bat, and its mouth is a gaping maw lined with elongated fangs that appear to be extrusions of the beak itself.

But there is something else even more unsettling about the creature than its appearance. It seems not to be quite there, for when you try to focus on it, its body appears blurred, as if it is out of focus or made from some incorporeal substance, such as mist or maybe smoke.

As the creature approaches from out of the night, it gives a screeching cry that can be clearly heard inside the cult's meeting place and sounds as if it foretells the doom of all those within. With every beat of the avian's wings comes another shocking revelation. For riding on the back of the great beast is a man.

"Dr Waugh," hisses Dr Blaine at your side. "He's not been idle either."

But the worst is yet to come. As you and everyone else within the conservatory awaits the arrival of the errant astrophysicist, the Earth's obstruction of the sun's light becomes total, and the moon goes black.

Something immediately changes. The hole in the sky where the moon hangs appears to become exactly that: a hole. Where you know the moon hangs in orbit a quarter of a million miles above the Earth, all you can see now is a yawning void – not the void of space, but the void of a hole between realities. Where there should be the Earth's natural satellite there is now a gaping portal, an opening between your universe and another alien cosmos.

Within the gateway between realities, something moves. Something vast. An entity of claws, multiple distended jaws, and myriad eyes, emerging from the interstellar mists of planetary nurseries.

Make a self-control test. Roll one die, add your **WILLPOWER** and your **SANITY**. You may spend **1 RESOURCES** to roll two dice and pick the highest. What's the result?

Total of 10 or more: turn to **292**.
9 or less: turn to **37**.

13

There is no sign of Dr Waugh in his office and the only place you can think of looking for him is in the observatory proper. But you've already been there.

> If you want to make your way back through the building and return to the spot where you found the key, turn to **170**.
>
> If you would prefer to leave the Warren Observatory and search for an answer to this mystery elsewhere, turn to **140**.

The two of you skirt round the side of the house, hoping to find a casement that has been left ajar. Unfortunately, you find no such thing – the house is locked up tight. But you're not going to let that stop you.

Picking up a choice stone from a flowerbed that lies beneath a suitable window, you strike it against the bottom corner of the window. There is a sharp crack as the pane shatters. Carefully reaching through, you unhook the latch and swing the window open. But as you go to climb through it into the darkened room beyond, the academic holds back.

"Wait," he says, his voice tense. "You must cut through the eldritch wards as well as breach any physical barriers. Take out the knife."

You vacillate for a moment before doing as he says. The blade feels heavy in your hand and strangely warm, as if it were a living thing.

"Like this." He mimes the motions he wishes you to make with the ritual blade. You mimic his actions, and he visibly relaxes. But this only makes you feel more uneasy. What can be the nature of the promises he made that he can be kept from entering the property unless the mystical wards of protection that have been cast upon it are dispelled first?

"We may now proceed."

At the doctor's behest, you climb through the window. Amorphous black shapes loom at you out of the oppressive darkness, but they only prove to be a tallboy and a pair of wingback chairs. Finding the door to the room, you open it and emerge into the familiar surroundings of the house's interior. On the walls, there are the same scenes of the Arkham of a hundred years ago and the same rich velvet drapes.

But the pictures and soft furnishings are not the only familiar presence here. What need does the cult have for human guards when it has the creatures of the swarm to serve as sentries?

The furious buzzing of the creatures alerts you to their presence before you see them. Looking up proves to be a mistake. As a pair of huge ugly insects descends toward you, you see nightmarish, beetle-like wasps crawling about the architraves and plaster cornicing, like honeybees milling around the entrance to a hive.

"Trylogogs," Dr Blaine mutters under his breath.

It is apparent to you that the monstrous bugs are guarding the way to the pair of doors at the end of the hallway opposite the main entrance to the house.

He points toward the brass-handled double doors. "That is the way we must go."

"But we're not going to get in without a fight," you point out.

"Then fight we must!" declares your companion.

A light suddenly flares in his hand, seemingly without any obvious means to make it and the tinny tang of ozone fills the air. But rather than worry about what Dr Blaine is doing, you focus your attention on the approaching insects. You may spend **1 RESOURCES** at the start of each round to add 2 to your total for that round.

Round one: roll two dice and add your **COMBAT**. If you have the Weakness {**FEAR OF INSECTS**}, deduct 2. If the total is 15 or more, you win the first round.

Round two: roll two dice and add your **COMBAT**. If you have the Weakness {**FEAR OF INSECTS**}, deduct 2. If you won the first round, add 2. If your total is 15 or more, you win the second round.

Round three: roll two dice and add your **COMBAT**. If you won the second round, add 2. You may spend **1 RESOURCES** at the start of the round to add 2 to your total. If you have the Weakness {**FEAR OF INSECTS**}, deduct 2. If your total is 13 or more, you win the third round.

> If you win the third round, turn to **74**.
> If you lose the third round, turn to **20**.

16

Slamming yourself against the door with all the might you can muster, you are rewarded by the satisfying sound of the wood around the lock splintering. The door flies open, and you stumble out into the corridor again, blinking at the sudden brightness.

Your shoulder throbs from having been used as a battering-ram, but the elation you feel at having freed yourself means that you are able to put the bruised ache from your mind more easily. Lose - **1 HEALTH**.

> **Turn to 151.**

17

The impossible, ethereal entities driven off, you hurry to the doors of the Observatory only to find them locked and the lights off. The Art Nouveau building lies under a pall of silence and darkness. You can't waste any more time here if you want to get to the bottom of this mystery.

> Spend either **1 CLUE** or **1 RESOURCES** or take **+1 DOOM**. Then turn to **140** to search somewhere else.

18

Boldly, you climb the steps to the front door but then pause. The portal before you is made of plain dark wood but, in the light cast by the lamp, you can see phantom images within the grain, shapes like the bulbous, multi-faceted eyes of flies, the delicate tracery of membranous wings, and hundreds upon hundreds of twitching, hairy legs.

> If you want to knock on the door, to attract the attention of whoever is within, turn to **58**.
> If you would rather try the door to see if it is open without knocking first, turn to **34**.

19

Your fingerprints are taken – record your [INKY FINGERS] on your Character Sheet – and you soon find yourself locked in a holding cell in the depths of the Easttown Police Station with all the other ne'er-do-wells who have been arrested this evening. A man with a ragged beard buried in a heavy overcoat snores in one corner, while an elderly woman dressed in a long, patched dress and shawl sits on the bench, staring vacantly into the middle distance. From one comes an aroma of alcohol and worse, while the other projects an aura of faded splendor, her shawl, clothes, jewelry and even her face giving the impression that they were all gorgeous before impecunity and a life of hardship ravaged their beauty.

You resign yourself to a long wait before being able to speak with anyone who might be able to help you with your current predicament and take a seat on the bench beside the woman. Rather unsettlingly, she is muttering to herself.

"He doesn't trust that Professor Nidus, you know?" She looks at you then. "Her of the Life Sciences Department. Doesn't trust her one bit. And he's not too keen on that Dr Waugh either. He's an... oh, what do you call it... an as-tro-phy-si-cist," she says, breaking the word down into its component parts. "He works at the Warren Observatory but hardly ever leaves his office."

"Who doesn't?" you ask, unable to help yourself. "Trust them, I mean."

"Dr Blaine, of course," the old woman says with a chuckle, giving you a nudge with her elbow.

How does she know so much about Dr Blaine and his associates?

She suddenly grabs your hands in hers and her demeanor changes. She fixes you with a penetrating stare. "I see darkness in your future!"

You gasp at this rather unexpected turn of events. Her behavior both perturbs and intrigues you.

If you want to pull your hands away, turn to **99**.
If you want to leave them where they are and see what happens next, turn to **159**.

20

Despite your best efforts to fend off the trylogogs, there are simply too many of them. They swarm all over you, their multi-jointed legs tangling in your hair, their twitching antennae caressing your skin. But worst of all is when they cease their exploratory behavior and resume their aggressive approach.

A dozen venom-tipped barbs plunge into your body, injecting their lethal poison. The pain is excruciating, although it does not last long for soon the toxin overwhelms you and you slip into unconsciousness, unlikely to wake again.

The End.

21

By the time you arrive at Miskatonic University, night has spread its purple mantle over Arkham. The collegiate buildings are visible only as blocks of shadow, but with certain elements – such as entrances and windows – picked out by spots of artificial light, and even the occasional flickering oil lamp.

But one building is more brightly lit than any other – due to the presence of several police cars and other vehicles, their headlight beams on full – and that is the Science Building. Not only that, but a cordon has been erected around the entrance to the building, manned by a single police officer. Nearby, a huddle of people are in deep discussion. Three of the men are wearing the peaked caps and uniforms of the Arkham Police Department, while the last is a tall man wearing a long trench coat.

> If you have the {POLICE} or {DETECTIVE} Ability, turn to **297**.

What do you want to do?

> Attempt to sneak past the police cordon and enter the building: turn to **61**.
> Talk to the policemen: turn to **81**.

22

The room becomes filled with the muffled humming of the insects as more and more of them come to impossible life but remain impaled by the piercing pins. Your awareness of what is happening is another strain on your already beleaguered mind. You cannot bear to remain here a moment longer and, leaving the books and their secret knowledge behind, you flee from the room.

> Lose - **1 SANITY** and turn to **151**.

You start to search through the maps and papers covering the workstation. There is all manner of star charts, books of tables detailing planetary orbits, and a page of handwritten dates. It looks like your typical scholarly clutter or, equally, as if someone left in a hurry.

Make an investigation check. Roll one die and add your **INTELLECT**. You may spend **1 CLUE** to instead roll two dice and pick the highest. What's the result?

> Total of 7 or more: turn to **180**.
> 6 or less: turn to **7**.

You can't wait for whatever Dr Blaine has in mind to occur. He might have provided you with some of the clues, but you have unraveled this mystery yourself. You are beholden to no man, especially one who you are now convinced has ulterior motives of his own.

So, what do you want to do?

> See if you have something about your person that you could use against the Cult of Assimilation: turn to **48**.
> Attack the cultists: turn to **221**.
> Come up with some other strategy: turn to **109**.

The handle turns, the door opens, and you step through into a room of which the Explorer's Society of Arkham would be proud. This is clearly a map room. The huge Mercator's projection of the world that covers one entire wall alone would have told you that, but there are large atlases open on a long table in the middle of the room, and there is a plan chest against an adjacent wall. Standing on a turned ebony pedestal of its own, in one corner of the room next to the map wall, is an ornately decorated globe. Opposite it, on the right-hand side of the huge map, is an equally ornate celestial globe on a golden stand that shows the apparent positions of the stars in the sky.

Above the map of the world has been painted a quote from literature:

"There are more things in Heaven and Earth, Horatio, than are dreamt of in your philosophy."
HAMLET, ACT 1, SCENE 5.

You are alone in the map room so, what do you want to do now?

> Take a closer look at the Mercator's projection map: turn to **86**.
> Take a closer look at the globe of the Earth: turn to **44**.
> Take a closer look at the celestial globe: turn to **70**.
> Leave the room: turn to **151**.

26

Your travails this night have taxed you more than you realized. Despite adrenaline giving your beleaguered body a boost, it is not enough to allow you to get to safety. Exhausted, your body overwhelmed by what you have had to endure as much as your mind, you collapse before you can even make it out of the conservatory. But you do not witness the end when it comes, for by then you have been trampled underfoot by the battling cultists.

The End.

27

"Professor Nidus's office is on the second floor, beyond the Kafka Collection," Dr Christopher tells you. "Now, if you will excuse me, I have work to do. Please close the door on your way out."

Your audience with the entomologist is clearly at an end. Leaving his office, and pulling the door to as requested, you decide what to do next.

> If you want to make your way to Professor Nidus's office, turn to **298**.
> If you would prefer to leave the Science Building and pursue your investigations elsewhere, turn to **140**.

28

Leaving the study without further ado, you hurry back down the corridor, only to run into four police officers heading in your direction. They in turn are followed by a jittery-looking member of the university's secretarial staff.

"Stop!" the burly sergeant leading them shouts, and you do. Approaching you he says, "We've had reports of a disturbance. It's possible one of the professors has been attacked. Have you seen anything?"

You open your mouth to speak as two of the other cops push past you and charge through the still-open door into Dr Blaine's study.

"Sarge!" one of them shouts. "You're going to want to see this."

Turn to **262**.

29

Taking hold of the handle, you slam yourself bodily against the door. When it doesn't budge you try again, only harder this time.

Still the doorway remains closed to you, only now your arm is numb and there is an uncomfortable tingling sensation in your fingertips. Lose - **1 HEALTH** and - **1 COMBAT**.

"We're wasting time," snaps Dr Blaine unsympathetically.

Descending the steps, your companion hurries off along the gravel path that surrounds the house and disappears around a corner. Nursing your aching shoulder, you follow at a trot.

Turn to **15**.

Next to the storage units you find some gauze and a roll of bandages. You don't hesitate in pocketing them as you have an unpleasant feeling they might prove to be useful later.

Take **+1 RESOURCES** and the SECRET: *Hidden Two*.

What do you want to do?

Look for Dr Blaine's body among those on the trolleys: turn to **186**.

Search for the academic in one of the refrigerated compartments that lie behind the gleaming metal hatches: turn to **226**.

Leave the morgue without disturbing the dead any more than you have already: turn to **246**.

It is no good. No matter how hard you slam yourself against the door or tug on the handle, the door remains stubbornly closed. Unable to get out, you look for a light switch but find none. You do not remain alone in your prison, however, as you are joined by a furious buzzing that seems to come from within the walls themselves. When your captors finally deem to let you out, in readiness for the part you will play from now on in their unholy ritual, you will be a gibbering wreck, unable to refuse them, your mind having been fractured by that incessant, maddening buzzing.

The End.

32

Unable to accept what you are seeing, and yet the primitive part of your brain instinctively understanding that you are in terrible danger and all thoughts of finding Dr Waugh gone, you run from the Warren Observatory and set off back down Crane Hill.

You can only hope that whatever the wisp-winged things are, they do not see fit to pursue you for long or that you can outrun them.

> Lose - **1 WILLPOWER** and - **1 SANITY**, then turn to **140**.

33

The study is a mishmash of all manner of academic clutter, many piles of books and bundles of papers, but noticeably there are some models of curious-looking animals, what looks like the skull of one of the big cats in a dusty glass case, and the plaster cast of a footprint, but whether it is that of a great ape, a bear, or something else, you cannot tell.

Your attention is next drawn to an arrangement of framed photographs on the wall to your left. Among them is an academic certificate in an ornate, giltwood frame, declaring that Devlin Blaine has a Doctorate of Philosophy in Zoology.

Looking more closely at the photographs, you see that they all have one thing in common – they all feature the bearded gentleman currently spreadeagled in his chair behind the desk. He is receiving an award at a smart dinner in one of them, standing with other members of the faculty in some, and visiting the Canadian Rockies in another. There is no doubt in your mind now that the lifeless figure is indeed Dr Blaine. Take **+1 CLUE.**

On the same wall as the photographs is a large pinboard adorned with all manner of newspaper clippings, star charts, and hand-drawn sketches annotated with incomprehensible symbols. A large bookcase covers the entirety of the wall opposite the pinboard.

Trying to ignore the disturbing presence of the apparently dead Dr Blaine, where do you want to look first in the search for more information?

> The pinboard? Turn to **114.**
> The large bookcase? Turn to **94.**
> The desk? Turn to **63.**

34

The handle turns and the grand front door swings open. Beyond lies a palatial hallway, the splendor of which remains undiminished. The floor is polished Italian marble, the ceiling is white, stucco plaster, and the walls between are adorned with all manner of golden drapes and age-worn paintings, their colors muted by time and decay.

From the grand entrance hall, twin curving staircases rise to the second floor of the house, while a wide archway in front of you leads to a carpeted hallway of polished oak paneling.

> If you want to climb the stairs to the floor above, turn to **151**.
> If you want to pass beneath the arch, turn to **84**.

Dr Blaine is anxious that you press on, but he has led you a merry dance this night in one way or another and, making some flippant comment about not being able to work on an empty stomach, you hastily scour the shelves for something to eat, as well as anything else that may prove of use to you in confronting the cult.

There is a wheel of cheese and the end of a sourdough loaf that you help yourself to, and wash it all down with the contents of a half a bottle of claret. Take **+1 HEALTH** and **+1 WILLPOWER**.

You also find a large [**BREADKNIFE**] and a bottle of fine [**BRANDY**]. You may take **+1 RESOURCES** for either of these items. If you take both, take **+2 RESOURCES**.

> Turn to **54**.

36

A trolley has been left outside the door to the morgue with all manner of clinical items on it that immediately draw your eye.

> If you want to examine the contents of the trolley, turn to **66**.
> If you just want to enter the morgue proper, now you are here, turn to **156**.

37

You cannot tear your eyes from the void-beast that lurks beyond the hole in the sky. Just the knowledge that such a thing can exist, even in some far-flung dimension of its own, is enough to drive you one step closer to irredeemable madness. Take **-1 SANITY**.

> If you are in possession of [ARCHIBALD'S ACCOUNT], turn to **68**.
> If not, turn to **111**.

Bringing yourself upright again, you break eye-contact with the inescapable void and put burgeoning thoughts of cosmic entropy and the end of all things from your mind by focusing on the here and now.

You are seeking Dr Waugh, and so far, you have failed to find him. But you know what he was looking at through the telescope and you know how it made you feel. How would it make you feel if you gazed at that same empty spot in the sky, hour after hour, night after night?

> Take +1 **WILLPOWER** and +1 **CLUE** and turn to **170**.

You are searched before being taken to the cells. While the policemen who search you do not necessarily appreciate the value of everything in your possession, they understand the threat posed by a loaded firearm all too well and take it from you.

Strike the [**PISTOL**] from your Character Sheet and take -1 **RESOURCES**.

> Turn to **19**.

40

Many members of the Cult of Assimilation wear enchanted masks of human skulls upon their faces to eliminate their individuality in service to the swarm, and you are in danger of losing your sense of identity and free will the longer you keep it on.

Tearing the hideous mask from your face, you cast it on the ground. Strike the [SKULL MASK] from your Character Sheet but take +1 WILLPOWER.

You have just enough time to try something else before the cultists are upon you.

> If you want to use a [BRASS TELESCOPE] (if you have one), turn to **212**.
> If you want to use the {SORCERY} Ability (if you can), turn to **173**.
> If you do not have either of these things, or do not want to use them now, turn to **275**.

41

As you stand there, observing all the hustle and bustle, you see two attendants take a stretcher from a black van and carry it into the Science Building. There can be no doubt now that Dr Blaine is dead, but do you want to risk drawing attention to yourself now?

What do you want to do?

If you have the {POLICE} or {DETECTIVE}
Ability, turn to **297**.
Attempt to sneak past the police cordon and enter
the building: turn to **61**.
Stroll over to the policemen and engage them in
conversation: turn to **81**.

You seize a slight figure close to you and shout at the others
to stay back. However, you are rather taken aback when
the black-robed figures continue to advance toward you,
seemingly uncaring of their fellow's fate. Not only that, but
the cultist in your clutches starts to fight back. Your hostage
is not prepared to go quietly.

Make a wrestling test. Roll one die and add your
COMBAT. You may spend **1 RESOURCES** to roll two
dice and pick the highest. If you have the {AGILE} Ability,
add 1. What's the result?

Total of 8 or more: turn to **138**.
7 or less: turn to **108**.

43

You can barely believe what you are witnessing, and yet you are, with your own senses. You do not dare doubt their veracity. You manage to remain calm but back slowly toward the door regardless. You do not want to remain here a moment longer than is absolutely necessary, in case your mind starts to unravel. Take + 1 **WILLPOWER**.

Once you are outside the library again, you take several deep breaths to calm yourself as you consider your options.

> If you want to try the other door, turn to **25**.
> If you want to return to the main hallway, turn to **247**.

44

The globe is clearly quite old but has been carefully preserved. You can't help giving it a spin within its cradle. As it slows to a stop, you hear a soft click. It doesn't open to reveal a concealed drinks trolley, however.

What do you want to do now?

> Take a closer look at the Mercator's projection map: turn to **86**.
> Take a closer look at the celestial globe: turn to **70**.
> Leave the room: turn to **151**.

The jotter is filled with esoteric scribblings, executed in a careful hand, but all as unintelligible as they are beautifully written. Some pages are covered in picture script, but like nothing you have seen before, while others bear line after line of what looks like mirror writing but which, when reversed, still makes no sense.

And then there are the drawings. One appears to be that of a curious vessel shaped like a giant cicada and covered in more of the curious pictograms. Others appear to be anatomical illustrations but of things composed of malformed claws, distended jaws, and too many eyes. Just looking at the crude images makes you feel uneasy, as if one of those hideous things is reaching out to lay a claw on you even now. You tell yourself you are being silly, but glance over your shoulder anyway, just in case. Take ‑1 SANITY and +1 CLUE.

You dread to think what secrets the notebook contains, but you still feel an overwhelming urge to find out more, if only because of the strange behavior exhibited by the arguing academics. And you will remain ignorant of the truth unless you can find someone to help you decode the symbols within. When you think of arcane symbols, there is one place that springs to mind immediately.

If you want to take [DR BLAINE'S NOTEBOOK] to Ye Olde Magick Shoppe in Uptown, turn to 171.

If you want to chase after the academics in order to return the notebook to its rightful owner, turn to 75.

While you put up a valiant defense against the ethereal entities, you are unable to get the better of them. If you were to push on to the entrance to the observatory you doubt you would make it there alive. You suddenly feel bitterly cold, as if the curious creatures are somehow sapping all warmth from the surrounding area – and their prey! The only option you have is to turn tail and run, while you still can, and search elsewhere, hoping against hope that the insubstantial mist-creatures don't follow you.

> Take -1 **HEALTH** and +2 **DOOM**, and then turn to **140**. You may spend 1 **CLUE** or 1 **RESOURCES** to reduce the **DOOM** penalty by 1; spend 2 **CLUES** or 2 **RESOURCES** to avoid adding any **DOOM**.

47

"Yes, I know Dr Blaine," Dr Christopher replies. "Not well, but I know of him. He is part of the Department of Zoology. Actually, he came to see me not so long ago."

"Really?" you ask, your interest piqued. "What did he want to see you about?"

"He had some questions about an unusual species of wasp

he wanted help identifying. I have something of a reputation among my peers for being able to identify oddities – the weird and uncanny of the insect world."

"And were you able to help him?"

The entomologist hesitates before answering, his gaze drifting to whatever it is that lies covered by the cloth on the workbench behind him. "No. But that wasn't the strangest thing."

You barely dare ask the question, in case you risk bringing the man out of his reverie and have him clam up on you. But you ask it anyway. "What was?"

"He kept talking about an egg he was searching for, of all things."

Take the SECRET: *Egg Hunter.*

As Dr Christopher is in such a talkative mood, you decide to probe him further. But what do you want to ask him?

If you want to ask him about Professor Nidus, turn to **228**.

If you want to ask him what he's doing, turn to **67**.

48

Surrounded by the devotees of the Lord of Swarms, what could you possibly use to disrupt the cult's ritual and still get out of here alive yourself?

If you want to use a [SKULL MASK] (if you have one), turn to 73.

If you want to use a [BRASS TELESCOPE] (if you have one), turn to 212.

If you want to use the {SORCERY} Ability (if you can), turn to 173.

If you do not have any of these things, or do not want to use them now, turn to 275.

49

Visible chinks of light between closed shutters would seem to imply that there is someone at home, but you cannot see any obvious doormen, or other guardians on duty as you approach the house along the drive. Climbing the steps at the front of the house, you try the door but are not entirely surprised to find that it is locked.

"We must gain entry, and quickly," Dr Blaine hisses, glancing anxiously at the cloudless night sky.

You are committed to getting inside the house, but what do you propose to do now?

> If you want to use force to gain entry via the front door, turn to **29**.
>
> If you want to gain entry by breaking in through a window: turn to **15**.
>
> If you think there is something else you could try: turn to **236**.

50

Either due to some unknowable alignment of the stars or simply because Professor Nidus chose this spot to be the place, the ritual of summoning is tied to this location and the strange, cicada decorated vessel. Nothing you have seen would suggest that human sacrifice has been involved in summoning the Swarm God or Silenus – but perhaps human blood could be instrumental in stopping it.

Ignoring Dr Blaine, and barging past the battling cultists, you stumble up the steps to the top of the plinth, the Blade of Ark'at in your hand, the portal-vessel before you. Professor Nidus stands opposite you with a look of anger, surprise and downright bewilderment on her face. You lock eyes with her and – convinced now that nothing less will help – you bring the ritual dagger down sharply and plunge it into your chest.

There is a moment of freezing pain and then it is transmuted into a numbing warmth that slowly spreads throughout your body. You crumple to the ground and your eyes become heavy. You are dimly aware of Professor Nidus's shrieks of rage, but they seem muffled, as if coming from another room. They gradually fade as the thud of your failing heartbeat grows louder in your ears, even as it starts to slow.

But before it stops altogether, your eyes close and in that moment, you are rewarded with a vision of another god rising to power in Arkham. A colossal egg, its shell scaled and translucent, cracks and from it is born a creature so perfect in every aspect that to gaze upon it would drive a mortal mind mad.

The Child of Paradise, Magh'an Ark'at, has come into the world, and the unfaithful shall fall before its divine rampage.

Take the SECRET: *You Can't Make An Omelet Without Breaking Eggs.*

Final score: 0 stars.

The End.

Faced by such overwhelming odds, surely the best way to rid Arkham of the threat posed by the warring cults, and to keep yourself alive, is to let the two sides battle it out in a war of assured mutual self-destruction. But how can you ensure a favorable outcome for you and the people of Arkham?

Make a wisdom test. Roll one die and add your **INTELLECT**. You may spend **1 CLUE** to roll two dice and pick the highest. If you have the **{STUDIOUS}** Ability, add 1. What is the result?

> 8 or higher: turn to **172**.
> 7 or less: turn to **127**.

52

The window opens onto a slope of roof tiles. As you peer through it, out of the corner of your eye you see something that is darker than the encroaching dusk heading toward the ridge of the roof above and behind the protruding dormer window. Could it be the old man's attacker?

> If you want to risk climbing out onto the roof after whoever or whatever it was you just saw, turn to **102**.
> If you would prefer to check the body, if you haven't already, turn to **82**.
> If you would prefer to search the study in the hope of turning up something that might help you, turn to **33**.

53

Through the door, you find yourself in what is clearly a robing room. Like a church vestry, there is hanging room for what looks like dozens of robes. Most of the open wardrobes are empty, but there are a few [CULTIST ROBES] that haven't been collected. They look like monks' habits made of black cloth, with deep hoods. They are also long enough to cover the whole body, right down to the ankles.

If you want to persuade Dr Blaine that it might be wise to disguise yourselves before going any further, record the [CULTIST ROBES] on your Character Sheet.

Whatever you decide, there is no other way in or out of this room, other than the door you entered through, and so you leave the way you came and make for the double doors.

> Turn to 72.

54

Leaving the kitchens of the great house, consulting the map once more, you see that a servant's passage leads to a glass-domed space that stands at the heart of the house. Looking from the blueprint to your surroundings, you determine precisely where you are and where you need to go now. And so, you set off along the passageway.

Upon reaching the door at the far end, Dr Blaine takes hold of the handle and turns, pushing the door open a crack. You are immediately struck by the drone-like chanting coming from the space beyond as well as a startling compost heat. It smells like a tropical greenhouse. Joining Dr Blaine at the crack of the open door, you peer through it. What lies beyond would appear to be a conservatory. Lit by myriad bright lights, and packed with all manner of exotic plants, it is buzzing with insect life.

Beyond the construction of glass and cast-iron high above your head, a full moon bathes Abaddan House in cold light. The purpose-built flowerbeds and numerous terracotta pots of varying sizes that hold the plants mark out four quadrants of the circular conservatory. The spaces between are filled with black-robed cultists, all chanting the same hypnotic refrain over and over, while the insects that throng the air bring their own strange music to the monotonous incantation. You are horrified to see that many of the cultists are hidden behind masks that appear to have been fashioned from human skulls.

At the center of the conservatory is a raised stone plinth. Atop this stands another black-clad cultist only their hood has been thrown back and you see that it is the woman from the diner – Professor Nidus herself. She is leading the chant whilst holding her hands out over the mouth of a curious clay pot. It rests on top of a stone table in front of her and is also made of orange terracotta, but gives the impression of being far more ancient. The conical vessel has been decorated to look like a giant cicada and it is open at the top. At the same time, the body of the cicada is marked with crude symbols that look like they have been scratched into the clay with nothing more than the potter's fingernail.

"Come on," Dr Blaine whispers and slips through the door into the conservatory. Not knowing what else to do, you follow, and the door swings shut behind you.

Make a focus test. Roll one die and add your **WILLPOWER**. You may spend **1 RESOURCES** to roll two dice and pick the highest. If you have the {SORCERY} Ability, add 1. What's the overall result?

> Total of 8 or more: turn to **104**.
>
> 7 or less: turn to **144**.

The door opens and you enter what would appear to be a family portrait gallery. The walls of this room are crammed with framed paintings of various people, that cover all manner of ages, apparel, career paths, and eras. There are oil paintings of whiskered military men, dressed in uniforms dating from as far back as the American War of Independence, while watercolors of matronly women with unsmiling brushstroke faces, and charcoal likenesses of a gaggle of children look down at you as you explore the room.

One painting shows a figure in the mold of the heroic explorers of the late nineteenth century, but what really catches your eye is the curious terracotta pot he is holding like it's a silver rowing trophy. Take +1 CLUE and the SECRET: *Family Gallery.*

Pleased, but also slightly surprised, that you have not found anything more disturbing than a late seventeenth century painting of a Puritan matriarch within the gallery, you leave by the same way you came in and return to the corridor.

Where do you want to go from here?

To try the other door that is now opposite you, turn to **131**.

To make your way to the central hallway of the house, turn to **194**.

56

Many members of the Cult of Assimilation wear masks of enchanted human skulls upon their faces to eliminate their individuality in service to the swarm, and now that you have put one on your sense of identity is being subsumed by the will of the hive mind. The Cult of Ezel-zen-rezl is devoted to calling a nightmarish proliferation of insectile hordes into the world to assimilate all into the swarming hive. And now that is your desire too.

Lose - **1 WILLPOWER** and turn to **13**.

57

You know that space is a void, and that most of what lies between the various stars, planets, galaxies, and nebulae is vast, unimaginable tracts of nothingness, but this total absence of *anything* attests to something more than that. It is as if you have been given a glimpse of what is to come, a cruel vision of the end of the universe, of what will remain after the last star has been snuffed out.

You feel as if what you are witnessing is the inevitability of decay, the ultimate endpoint of entropy. No matter how you choose to spend your mayfly life, no matter what you hope to achieve or what forces you choose to oppose, in the end it will make no difference whatsoever. The death of the cosmos is inescapable. You feel consumed by an aching hollowness, as if the death of the universe has already begun, deep within your core, and that knowledge creates its own aching void inside your head.

Lose - **1 SANITY**, and then turn to **170**.

58

If you are going to knock on the door, you see no reason to be hesitant about it.

Taking the tarnished brass knocker in hand, you strike

it against the smoothed indentation in the wood beneath it firmly three times. You believe you hear the reverberation of your summons echo through the hallways of the house beyond and then wait. But when no one comes to see who is waiting outside, you consider it might be time for a different approach.

If you want to try to open the door, turn to **34**.
If you want to leave the porch and creep around to the side of house, in search of an alternative way in, turn to **120**.

On reaching the Police Station, you are rough-handed until you are standing in front of the custody sergeant ready to be processed and charged, before finally being locked up. Unfortunately, no one seems interested in hearing your side of the story and your claims of innocence, and simply being in the wrong place at the wrong time, go unheeded.

If you have a [PISTOL], turn to **39**.
If not, turn to **19**.

Returning to Dr Waugh's office, you slip the key into the lock and feel a frisson of delight pass through you when it turns, and you are able to open the door. Take the SECRET: *Hidden Five.*

The Warren Observatory may be the newest building on campus, but the astrophysicist's office still resembles something that would not be out of place in the older, nineteenth century buildings, filled as it is with all manner of scientific paraphernalia. You have the distinct impression that no one on the academic staff at Miskatonic University ever throws anything away.

On the opposite side of the room are several large windows, through which you can see myriad stars. Moonlight bathes everything in its monochrome luminescence. To your left is a wall of bookcases and to your right, a wall covered in star maps of the heavens as well as diagrams of the orbits of the planets and the like.

However, in the middle of the room, resting on top of a couple of tables that have been pushed together, is the most incredible model of the town of Arkham. As far as you can tell it is to scale, with terrain sculpted from clay surmounted by tiny model buildings constructed from balsa wood and found objects. It looks like it should be the setting for someone's model railway, only it is far more impressive than that and there is no train.

Roll one die and add your **INTELLECT**. You may spend **1 CLUE** to roll two dice and pick the highest. What's the result?

> Total of 7 or more: turn to **243**.
> 6 or less: turn to **293**.

61

You sidle up to the piece of rope that has been used to cordon off the entrance to the Life Sciences Department and, when the rookie who is on duty has his back turned, slip underneath it and into the building.

You do not get very far before you hear rapid footsteps behind you, and you feel a firm hand on your shoulder.

"Stop right there!" It is the man wearing the trench coat. He whips out his badge and you need the name upon it. "Who are you and what business do you have here?" Detective Harden asks. "You saw the rope, right? You know you just crossed a police line?"

You are going to have to think fast if you are to come up with a convincing excuse.

Make a quick-thinking test. Roll one die and add your INTELLECT. You can spend 1 CLUE to roll two dice and pick the highest. If you have the {QUICK-WITTED} Ability, add 1. What's the result?

> Total of 7 or more: turn to **101**.
> 6 or less, or if you don't have [DR BLAINE'S NOTEBOOK]: turn to **81**.

62

The first proper evidence you have that you are not alone is the air that buffets you with the rhythm of wingbeats. The second warning you have that you are in danger is the ominous silhouette that blocks the light from the moon when you look up to see what is creating the eddies in the air.

What you see descending from the sky sends a chill down your spine. It possesses both human and inhuman qualities. Its body is like that of a malnourished man, but the wings, horns, tail, and deepest green-black skin are like something out of a nightmare. But worst of all is the total absence of any facial features – the thing doesn't even have a mouth.

Take - **1 SANITY** and the SECRET: *Hunting Nightgaunt*.

And then it swoops down, claws outstretched, ready to attack! It is going to take everything you have, in terms of nerve as well as physical strength, to get through your latest trial. You may spend 1 **RESOURCES** at the start of each round to add 2 to your total for that round.

Round one: roll two dice and add your **COMBAT** and your **WILLPOWER**. If the total is 15 or more, you win the first round.

Round two: roll two dice and add your **COMBAT** and your **WILLPOWER**. If you won the first round, add 2. If your total is 16 or more, you win the second round.

Round three: roll two dice and add your **COMBAT** and your **WILLPOWER**. If you won the second round, add 2. If your total is 17 or more, you win the third round.

If you won at least two rounds, turn to **103**.
If you lost at least two rounds, turn to **83**.

You feel uncomfortable rummaging through the objects on Dr Blaine's desk when his body is still limp in the chair beside you, but you need answers. But rather than answers, all you uncover are more questions. In one drawer you find a [LIGHTER], in another a loaded [PISTOL], and in another, a half-empty bottle of [WHISKEY]. If you want to take any of these items, record them on your Character Sheet and take +1 RESOURCES for each item taken.)

As you look up from the desk, you believe you glimpse movement outside the window, even though you are on the third floor.

Where do you want to look next in your quest for answers?

The pinboard? Turn to **195**.
The large bookcase? Turn to **175**.
Through the open window? Turn to **134**.
Somewhere other than Dr Blaine's study? Turn to **215**.

You remain frozen where you are as the wraithlike creatures swoop toward you. You can see them more clearly now – the impression of gaping beaks, mist-trailing tails, and smoky talons. Their intention is clear. It is as if they consider that you have trespassed here, and they cannot let such hubris go unpunished. You have no choice but to prepare for battle. But how can you battle something that appears to be little more than sentient smoke?

You may spend **1 RESOURCES** at the start of each round to add 2 to your total for that round.

Round one: roll two dice and add your **COMBAT** and your **WILLPOWER**. If you have the **{SECRET RITES}** Ability, add 1. If the total is 15 or more, you win the first round.

Round two: roll two dice and add your **COMBAT** and your **WILLPOWER**. If you have the **{SECRET RITES}** Ability, add 1. If you won the first round, add 2. If your total is 16 or more, you win the second round.

> If you won the second round, turn to **113**.
> If you lost the second round, turn to **133**.

65

Unfortunately, the sepulchral atmosphere of this place and your current state of mind make you unusually suspicious of someone demonstrating such apparent kindness. She must have some ulterior motive, surely.

Make a paranoia test. Roll one die and add your **WILLPOWER**. You can spend **1 RESOURCES** to roll two dice and pick the highest. If you have the Weakness {CURSED}, deduct 1. If you have the Weakness {HAUNTED}, deduct 1 as well. What's the result?

> Total of 9 or more: turn to **118**.
> 8 or less: turn to **89**.

66

On the trolley is a large bottle of [SWABBING ALCOHOL], a clipboard, a [BONESAW], a bloodstained apron, and a bottle of pills.

> If you want to take a closer look at the clipboard, turn to **126**.
> If you want to take a closer look at the pills, turn to **96**.
> If you want to enter the morgue, turn to **156**.

Dr Christopher half glances at the workbench behind him, and whatever it is that lies beneath the cloth. "I am a Professor of Entomology. From time to time I must examine bizarre specimens for purposes of scholarship and classification."

He makes no move to reveal what it is he has been working on. Neither does he seem inclined to elaborate on what his role entails. Is there anything you can say that will encourage him to be open up to you?

Make a quick-thinking test. Roll one die and add your **INTELLECT**. You may spend **1 CLUE** to roll two dice and pick the highest. If you have the **{QUICK-WITTED}** Ability, or the **{STUDIOUS}** Ability, add 1. What's the result?

> Total of 7 or more: turn to **117**.
> 6 or less: turn to **147**.

You recall reading about this impossible entity in Archibald Nidus's notebook, and in that moment realize you have no reason to doubt that anything contained within its accursed pages is true. While ignorance may be bliss, a little knowledge is a dangerous thing! Take +1 **INTELLECT**.

While the arrival of the abomination with the errant Dr Waugh astride its back may be the most incredible thing you have witnessed this night, it is not the only incredible thing. Right now, between you and Dr Waugh's semi-corporeal steed, you can see figures crawling over the glass panels of the conservatory roof – dozens of them!

Professor Nidus's shrieking is suddenly silenced by the simultaneous shattering of a hundred panes of glass, and the astrophysicist's followers drop into the conservatory, heedless of their own safety. For they have seen what Dr Waugh has seen, which means that these nihilistic stargazers know, deep within their bones, that they are doomed no matter what and so have eradicated all fear of injury from their minds. The two cults are evidently rivals and clearly each intends to ensure that it is their particular god that rises to power in Arkham this night, but which do you consider to be the greater threat?

What do you want to do?

Confront the Cult of Assimilation: turn to **281**.
Attack the cultists of the Empty Sky: turn to **201**.
Stand back at see what happens: turn to **181**.

In no time at all, you are standing at the bottom of the drive leading up to the Abaddan House once more. In fact, you are not entirely sure how you got here so quickly, only that your memory of the journey here is a blur. Dr Blaine is watching you with an unsettling look of gleeful interest, like a scientific researcher observing a rat in a maze.

"How did we get here so–" you begin to ask.

"Time is of the essence," Dr Blaine's interrupts. "All that matters is that we are here. But now we must enter the house."

Having been here already tonight, what do you want to suggest as the best way of getting in?

> By the front door: turn to **49**.
> Break in through a side window: turn to **15**.
> Try something else: turn to **236**.

The celestial globe is a magnificent piece. You turn it with care, wondering at the way the constellations have been depicted as gods and monsters of classical myth. You suddenly find yourself unable to rotate the globe any further and hear a distinct click.

What do you want to do now?

Take a closer look at the Mercator's projection map:
turn to **86**.
Take a closer look at the globe of the Earth: turn to
107.
Leave the room: turn to **151**.

Rattling the door handle furiously to no effect, uncaring of
who might hear you now, you slam your shoulder into the
door. It remains stubbornly shut but you imagine it gave
a little under the impact. You try again, applying greater
force this time. While the door remains sealed, you hear
what sounds like metal screws pulling within the wood
fiber.

Make a strength test. Roll one die and add your
COMBAT. You may spend **1 RESOURCES** to roll two
dice and pick the highest. What's the result?

Total of 8 or more: turn to **16**.
7 or less: turn to **31**.

Putting a hand to one of the doors, Dr Blaine opens it cautiously. You are immediately struck by the drone-like chanting coming from the space beyond as well as a startling compost heat. It smells like a tropical greenhouse. Joining Dr Blaine at the crack of the open door, you peer inside. What lies beyond would appear to be a conservatory. Lit by myriad bright lights, and packed with all manner of exotic plants, it is buzzing with insect life.

Beyond the construction of glass and cast-iron high above your head, a full moon bathes Abaddan House in cold light. The purpose-built flowerbeds and numerous terracotta pots of varying sizes that hold the plants mark out four quadrants of the circular conservatory. The spaces between are filled with black-robed cultists, all chanting the same hypnotic refrain over and over, while the insects that throng the air bring their own strange music to the monotonous incantation.

At the center of the conservatory is a raised stone plinth. Atop this stands another black-clad cultist. Their hood has been thrown back and you see that it is the woman from the diner – Professor Nidus herself. She is leading the chant whilst holding her hands out over the mouth of a curious clay pot. It rests on top of a stone table in front of her that is also made of orange terracotta but gives the impression of being far more ancient. The conical vessel has been decorated to look like a giant cicada and it is open at the top. At the same time, the body of the cicada is marked with crude symbols that look like they have been scratched into the clay with nothing more than the potter's fingernail.

"Come on," Dr Blaine whispers and slips through the door into the conservatory. Not knowing what else to do, you follow.

As the doors swing shut again behind you, heads turn in your direction. You are horrified to see that many of them are hidden behind masks that appear to have been fashioned from human skulls.

> If you are wearing [CULTIST ROBES], turn to 124.
> If not, turn to 144.

73

You brandish the mask before the advancing cultists and realize it is like those worn by some of them. Not knowing what else to do, in desperation you put the mask on. The cultists come to an abrupt halt and watch as your body is suddenly seized by some kind of paralysis. The chanting fills your head, but now you feel compelled to join in with the buzzing mantra.

Make a willpower test. Roll one die and add your **WILLPOWER**. You may spend **1 RESOURCES** to roll two dice and pick the highest. If you have the {SORCERY} Ability, add 1. What's the result?

> Total of 10 or more: turn to **40**.
> 9 or less: turn to **56**.

74

The hornet-like horrors drop out of the air, some of them smoking, their bodies burnt to a crisp by the esoteric powers Dr Blaine appears to have at his disposal. The blade was just as effective at stopping the creatures and the rush of exhilaration you felt battling the bugs still hums through every nerve and fiber of your body.

Dr Blaine doesn't hesitate in throwing open the double doors and you hurry after him before more of the monstrous insects make an appearance, closing the doors firmly behind you. You are in another passageway, this one much shorter than the last. To your left is a single unadorned door that has been left slightly ajar, while in front of you is a second set of double doors. You are startled when you hear a buzzing drone again and fear another attack from the trylogogs. It takes you a moment to realize it isn't the droning of insects you can hear but the droning of human voices, coming from beyond the next portal.

"The ceremony has already begun," hisses Dr Blaine, making for the double doors.

But now it is your turn to advise caution. "Is such a direct approach wise?" you ask him. "We are only two and will be sorely outnumbered by Professor Nidus and her followers."

Dr Blaine turns to face you. "Then what do you suggest?"

Quickly scanning the corridor, you consider your options, but they are sadly lacking. There is the matter of the door to your left, however.

> If you want to see what lies beyond the open door, turn to **53**.
> If you want to follow Dr Blaine's lead and advance to the next set of doors, turn to **72**.

Having already packed away your personal possessions, you exit the diner. It is late afternoon and there is an unseasonal chill in the air. Looking left and right along the street, you catch sight of the two academics walking away from each other in opposite directions. Opening the notebook again, in the hope that it might provide you with inspiration regarding who to follow, you see something written inside the front cover, in the top right-hand corner of the first page:

Property of Dr Blaine, Zoology Department,
School of Life Sciences, Miskatonic University

> If you want to follow the older gentleman, turn to **197**.
> If you want to try to catch up with the elderly woman, turn to **98**.

Unable to overcome your natural curiosity, you lean forward and put your eye to the eyepiece. You do not touch any of the sensitive knurled calibration controls but wait for a moment.

At first, you think your eye has not yet adjusted to the focus as you can see nothing through the viewfinder, but blinking and waiting doesn't make any difference. You look up to check that the dome is open and that the telescope is indeed pointing at the night sky. Only then do you peer into the viewfinder again, but still, you can see nothing. There are no clouds obscuring this patch of sky at present and you would expect to see a smattering of stars, if not the planets or even a shooting star. The total absence of anything makes you uneasy.

Make a self-control test. Roll one die and add your **WILLPOWER**. You may spend **1 RESOURCES** to roll two dice and pick the highest. What's the result?

> Total of 8 or more: turn to **38**.
> 7 or less: turn to **57**.

Dr Blaine poses the greatest threat. You can see that now. He has been hiding in plain sight all along. You can feel the power emanating from him now that he has revealed his true self. As he glides through the domed conservatory, striking down all before him, he suddenly turns to regard you, as if sensing what you are intending. You immediately feel yourself wither. Dr Blaine has some esoteric hold over you that it will take a tremendous effort of will to overcome – but overcome it you must.

Make a magical resistance test. Roll one die and add your **WILLPOWER**. You may spend **1 RESOURCES** to roll two dice and pick the highest. If you have the {**SECRET RITES**} Ability, add 1. If you have the {**SORCERY**} Ability, add 2. However, if you have the Weakness {**CURSED**}, deduct 1. What's the result?

Total of 10 or more: turn to **218**.
9 or less: turn to **280**.

As you open the hatch, the droning hum becomes suddenly louder, and you are assailed by an appalling smell. There must be flies inside the compartment, no doubt laying their eggs in the poor unfortunate who lies within.

Warily, you slide out the drawer, within which lies the body of a man you recognize. And yet, at the same time, his features have become almost unrecognizable. The gray hair and beard are the same, and the clothes are those of the man you saw arguing with the spiky woman in Velma's Diner. But the melted features are nothing like those of the individual you encountered earlier.

The way the sleeves of his jacket and his trouser legs have crumpled gives the impression that there is no longer anything supporting them from within. But it is the man's face that is the worst. The way his features have collapsed inwards makes it look like someone has taken a blowtorch to a waxwork.

You are distracted from the horror of the dead man's appearance by the buzzing which slowly rises in intensity. You take a small, startled step back as something moves within one crumpled sleeve of the jacket, heading toward the man's chest. For a moment all is still and then something like a cross between a hornet and a bluebottle crawls out from under the unbuttoned jacket.

Unable to take your eyes off the horrible thing, you see more of the grotesque insects emerge from within the man's clothes. What shakes you from your reverie is the moment one of the critters crawls out of the ruin of the man's melted mouth.

Make a composure test. Roll one die and add your **WILLPOWER**. You may spend **1 RESOURCES** to roll two dice and pick the highest. What's the result?

> Total of 9 or more: turn to **110**.
> 8 or less: turn to **80**.

Wondering what other celestial phenomena might be covered in the other volumes in the series, you start to flick through the books still on the shelf. However, it is not another title about astronomy that catches your attention – it is a postcard that has been used as a bookmark in one of the tomes that falls onto the reading desk as you move the hardbacks around on the shelf.

The image on the front is that of some ancient, stepped pyramid emerging from a thick jungle. However, written on the back in a barely legible sloping hand is a much more intriguing message:

Believe we are not far from the location of the vessel now.
Will write again when I have more news.
Praise be to the Lord of the Swarms. Praise be to Ezel-
zen-rezl!
Yours, Archibald

Take **+1 CLUE** and **+1 INTELLECT**, and the SECRET: *Hidden Six*.

> Turn to **9**.

You feel distinctly threatened by the presence of the insects and dread to think what might happen next. Take -1 **SANITY**, and the Weakness {**FEAR OF INSECTS**}.

> Turn to **110**.

You tell the policemen that you are here to see Dr Blaine, but the mere mention of his name has them regarding you with suspicion. Feeling your face redden in embarrassment, you try to bluster your way out of your tricky situation but become tongue-tied as the cops interrogate you on the details of your less-than-convincing story. The more you talk, the more you can see the suspicion deepen on the policemen's faces.

Before you know it, you are being handcuffed as you suddenly find yourself at the top of the list of suspects in the murder of Dr Devlin Blaine. There is little point trying to escape when the university campus is already swarming with police, so you allow yourself to be led away and bundled into one of the cars, hoping that you will be able to sort this mess out down at the Police Station.

> Take the Weakness {**CRIMINAL**} and turn to **59**.

The man doesn't move as you approach, and you feel a chill creep up your spine. Is he dead? His eyes are closed, and you cannot see any obvious signs that he is breathing. However, neither can you see any obvious signs of injury.

Steeling yourself, you reach a hand toward his exposed throat and press the tips of your fingers against his neck. You cannot feel a pulse under the clammy skin.

The door to the study suddenly bangs behind you, and you snatch your hand away as four cops bundle into the room, followed by a jittery-looking secretary.

"Hands in the air!" the burly sergeant leading the cops shouts, and you do as he says. His eyes flick between you and the body in the chair, and appalled horror creeps across his face with what feels like glacial sluggishness.

Turn to **262**.

It is no good – what can you, a mere mortal, do against such an obscene horror? Your nerve is the first to break, and then your body, as the gaunt creature rakes you with its razor-sharp claws. Whoever eventually finds your body will wonder what could have possibly done this to you. But this being Arkham, no one will search very hard or very long for the answer.

The End.

84

Your echoing footsteps become muffled as you pass from the marble hallway to the carpeted corridor, which in turn gives way to a crossing of the ways within the house. Corridors decorated with more thick carpets and walnut paneling lead off to the east and west wings of the house, while before you stands a pair of impressive double doors.

You pause, ears straining, and imagine you can hear a distant susurrus, a whispering sound coming from somewhere deeper in the house.

Which way do you want to go from here?

> If you want to see where the left-hand corridor takes you, turn to **176**.
> If you want to try the corridor to the right, turn to **234**.
> If you want to approach the double doors, turn to **267**.

85

Opening the door, you find yourself at the entrance to a grand private library. A large lamp on a reading desk suffuses the room in a soft orange glow. The desk stands against the middle of one wall. On either side of it are floor-to-ceiling bookcases, while on the opposite wall narrower bespoke bookcases are interspersed with framed displays of butterflies, moths, beetles, and all manner of other winged insects. Every selection of specimens is pinned to a white card and kept behind glass, like precious jewels or embroidered treasures.

Like the rest of the house, the library is devoid of life but gives the impression of someone having been in here not long before you arrived. You notice that several books have been left open on the reading desk. As you are alone, you approach the table and see what it was that the last person to visit the library had been reading.

The largest book has a green binding and bears the title *An Atlas of the Americas* impressed into the spine in gold. Next is a smaller, black volume that merely bears the Roman numerals *VII* on the cover. You are excited to see that the last book is a notebook, its pages covered in a neat but barely legible sloping script.

What do you want to do now?

Read the green book: turn to **164**.
Thumb through the black-bound book: turn to **187**.
Peruse the handwritten notebook: turn to **207**.
Leave the library and try the other door off the corridor: turn to **25**.
Return to central hallway of the house: turn to **247**.

You take in the continents of the Earth at a distance and then approach the painting, marveling at the detail that has gone into it. Arkham has even been demarcated on the north-east coast of America with a large red dot.

However, up close you can see a vertical line where the painting has been cut. It is too straight and precise to have been accidental damage and using your fingers you trace the thin gap to where it turns right. It looks like you have found a hidden door – but you can find no obvious means of opening it, no matter where you press on the painting or how hard you try.

What do you want to do now?

Take a closer look at the globe of the Earth: turn to **44**.
Take a closer look at the celestial globe: turn to **70**.
Leave the room: turn to **151**.

You open door #87 and slide out the stainless steel pallet. But there is no body lying upon it. Is that why the name scrawled next to #87 on the clipboard was crossed out, because the body has been moved? But to where? And why?

Gain the Weakness {**PARANOID**} and take the SECRET: *Hidden One*.

At least it isn't Dr Blaine's body that's been taken. Or at least you hope not.

Standing there in the silence of the morgue, you become aware of a buzzing sound. It sounds like it's coming from behind another of the stainless steel doors.

> If you want to risk opening the door in question, turn to **78**.
> If you want to leave the morgue without further delay, turn to **246**.

88

"I will help you," you tell Dr Blaine, whilst also harboring concerns regarding his personal motivations in this matter. However, you are in too deep to back out now. Aware of the danger Arkham is in, you have no choice but to help. "But the blade remains in my possession."

For a moment, from the look in the academic's eyes, you fear that Dr Blaine may take steps to steal the knife from you, but then the stormy expression passes. He says calmly, "Very well."

He rises stiffly and gestures for you to follow him. Warily, you do so as he leaves the warmth of the diner for the cold and darkness of the night beyond its railcar walls.

As the two of you set off for French Hill, Dr Blaine says, "The Cult of Assimilation has acquired the means to bring their god into this world, from where it waits in droning darkness."

"And Professor Nidus is the head of cult?" you ask.

"Here in Arkham, yes. They are dangerous, all of them. They worship Ezel-zen-rezl, the Lord of Swarms. The Ezel-zen-rezl hive seeks to assimilate all organic life into itself and its human devotees are working for it to achieve that goal. The weak-minded fools believe assimilation into the swarm to be an honor. Can you imagine?"

Your skin crawls at the thought of thousands of insect bodies scuttling all over you.

"The cult plans to unleash the swarm upon Arkham, and they will do so this very night unless we stop them."

Turn to **69**.

Perhaps it's the oppressive atmosphere of the library. Maybe it's the way the woman is smiling at you, so sincerely. Or perhaps it's just a reflection of your own state of mind. But no matter the truth, you cannot bring yourself to spend another moment with the librarian. Instead, you mutter something about not needing any help and disappear into the stacks.

Not really knowing where to start, it is more by luck than judgment that you end up in the local history section where you find a book about a once famous explorer who called Arkham home some fifty years ago. But the thing that you find most intriguing is that his name was Archibald Nidus. Take **+1 CLUE.**

You could lose yourself in the library for weeks, but you have a sneaking suspicion that time is of the essence if you are to get to the bottom of the mystery surrounding the fate of Dr Blaine. It's time to continue your search for clues elsewhere.

> Lose either **1 CLUE** or **1 RESOURCES**, or take **+1 DOOM.** Then turn to **140.**

You descend the black metal staircase at a stumbling run, holding onto the rail the whole way down. Upon reaching the bottom, you see four cops have bundled out of the cars and are making for the main entrance to the building.

> If you want to approach the police, with the intention of talking to them, turn to **242.**
> If you would rather not draw attention to yourself and want to flee the scene, turn to **202.**

Breathing deeply to slow your racing pulse, you turn from the door and cautiously creep further into the room. You follow the wall, keeping one hand in contact with the flocked wallpaper, caressing its subtly embossed surface, hoping to find a light switch. You take small steps, so as not to hurt yourself should you come across a piece of furniture that has been hidden from you by the darkness.

But rather than a switch, the first thing your hand finds is a wooden picture frame – at least that's what you think it is to begin with. As you draw your fingertips across it, however, you find that the frame is rather thick for a watercolor or oil painting and is inset with a pane of glass. In fact, now you think about it, it feels more like a box.

In the dark-muffled stillness of the room you hear the faintest, briefest buzzing of wings, and the glass of the wall-mounted display case vibrates in sympathy under your touch.

You immediately snatch your hand away, as if instinctively fearing something might harm you. But you remain where you stand, listening intently. The sound comes again. It seems to be coming from behind the glass. Is there a fly or something similar trapped inside the case?

Then a second set of buzzing wings, the sound subtly different from the first, joins it in a disquieting counterpoint. And then a third, and a fourth, and a fifth. The buzzing becomes steadily louder and more intense and you start to wonder if there is an entire swarm of bees trapped behind the glass. The darkness was merely your prison before, but now it has taken on a more threatening quality, filling your mind with all manner of illogical fears. Take ‑1 **SANITY** and the Weakness {**CLAUSTROPHOBIA**}.

It is no good, you cannot stay here a moment longer. You must get out!

> Turn to **71**.

92

The arrival of the rival cult has thrown the followers of Ezel-zen-rezl into disarray, but it has also made them desperate, and therefore dangerous. The pair you are battling against bludgeon you with their fists and when you end up on the ground, they continue their assault. You try to cry out through bloodied lips, but all the breath has been knocked from your body by their savage attack.

> Lose ‑2 **HEALTH** and turn to **181**.

What do you have that you think might be effective against these ethereal entities?

> If you have the {SORCERY} Ability and want to use it now, turn to **153**.
>
> If you have a [BLACK TALON] and want to use it now, turn to **183**.
>
> If you have a [BRASS TELESCOPE] and want to use it now, turn to **203**.
>
> If you have a [PISTOL] and want to use it now, turn to **223**.
>
> If you have none of these things, or do not want to use them now, take -**1 RESOURCES** and turn to **64**.

94

The bookcase is a veritable treasure trove of esoteric literature. There is one ancient tome concerning *Alliances and Enmities Among the Outer Gods*, another called *The Gospel of Ark'at*, and a third which is a guide to translating ancient languages. If you want to take this guide, gain the {ANCIENT LANGUAGES} Ability.

Turning from the shelves, your gaze falls on the open

window once more, and you can't help wondering if something came or left through it, and whether that is the reason for Dr Blaine's current unfortunate state.

Where do you want to look next in your quest for answers?

The pinboard? Turn to **195**.
The desk? Turn to **154**.
Through the open window? Turn to **134**.
Somewhere other than Dr Blaine's study? Turn to **215**.

95

As you set off for the affluent and ancient neighborhood of French Hill, you begin to feel uneasy – more uneasy than you have felt so far this evening, as if something watches you from the darkness.

If you have the Weakness {CURSED}, add +1 to your total **DOOM**. If you have the Weakness {HAUNTED}, add +1 to your total **DOOM**. And if you have the Weakness {PARANOID}, add +1 to your total **DOOM**.

What is your total **DOOM**?

3 or more: turn to **62**.
2 or less: turn to **11**.

The pills are caffeine tablets, the kind that are sometimes used by doctors to get them through long nightshifts at the hospital. If you want to take the pills with you, take **+1 RESOURCES**.

Choosing something you haven't tried already, what do you want to do now?

> Take a closer look at the clipboard: turn to **126**.
> Enter the morgue: turn to **156**.

It would seem most sensible to you to look for Dr Waugh in the dome, especially if he was booked in to use the telescope this evening. Making your way through the observatory you soon find yourself standing inside the observatory proper. A grand, wrought iron staircase leads up to the platform on which stands the impressive telescope.

There is a distinct chill in the air because the dome is partially open so that the night sky can be viewed through the telescope. A clattering sound sends you climbing the staircase to the telescope platform, but there is no one there. There is a workstation next to the telescope – a desk strewn with charts, pieces of paper covered in scribbled notes, and slim pamphlets – and you can't shake the feeling that someone has been here recently.

> If you want to make a thorough search of the area, to see what you might be able to find, turn to **23**.
> If you want to look through the viewfinder of the telescope while you are here, turn to **76**.

You set off in pursuit, but before you can catch up with her, the woman hails a taxicab. You call out but your entreaty for her to stop is lost as the driver revs the Checker's motor. You can only watch helplessly as she climbs in and the cab pulls away from the sidewalk.

The only way you're going to be able to follow the woman now is if you hail a ride yourself.

> If you want to hail a cab, turn to **128**.
> If you would rather change your mind and go after the old man instead, turn to **167**.

99

You try to pull free of the old woman's grasp, but she only tightens her grip.

"No, you must hear what I have to say!" she hisses.

> If you want to yank your hands free of her clutches, turn to **119**.
> If you want to hear her out, turn to **159**.

100

Despite the taxing travails you have suffered this night, much-needed adrenaline gives your body the kick it needs, and you flee from Abaddan House, the cries of the battling cultists and the droning voice of the swarm fading into the distance.

But as you retrace the route you took to get here and find yourself outside, swaddled by the cold night air once more, something unbelievable and world-warping occurs. As you continue to flee through the grounds, you feel tremors under your feet and a sudden drop in air pressure, all of which is accompanied by the howling of a hurricane. Risking no more than a glance over your shoulder, in that moment you witness what is happening to the house. The mansion appears to be collapsing. Impossible geometries take hold of the building as it begins to fold in on itself, brick walls bending, pitched roofs buckling, and windows shattering in their frames, and those same apertures are crushed shut.

You do not stop running, but increase your effort, panic driving you to exhaustion. Moonlight chases you as the eclipse passes and you look to the sky to see the moon has returned, the hole in the sky and the entity that lurked beyond it, both having vanished. Fatigued, your legs and lungs burning, you stumble to a halt and gaze across the moonlit estate. But of Abaddan House there is no sign. There is not even a footprint on the ground where it previously stood, no sign of a basement or wine cellar. Nothing at all but a sweep of untouched turf. It is as if the house never existed at all. In fact, your memories of the place are already starting to evaporate.

Other things are no longer as clear as they once were in your mind. You remember Dr Blaine and something to do with his academic rivals, but you cannot recall what the source of their disagreement was. You first encountered them in Velma's Diner. That's right. Perhaps if you were to return there now you would recall what brought you to this area of parkland within the French Hill district of Arkham in the middle of the night. Take - **1 SANITY**.

As you set off for the diner once more, tentacle-like tendrils of black cloud crawling across the heavens, an unconscious niggle at the back of your mind tells you that something's not right, but you cannot remember what...

Take the SECRET: *Remember, Remember.*

Final score: 1 star.

The End.

"... And so, I had to find out what was going on, because I was hoping to return this to Dr Blaine," you conclude, risking all and showing Detective Harden the notebook.

He opens it, checks the inscription inside the front cover, and then flicks through the hand-scrawled pages.

"Looks like it's written in some sort of code, if you ask me," says the detective.

"That's what I thought," you reply.

"Well good luck decoding it now. After all, I'm afraid Dr Blaine's not going to be much help."

"And why is that?" you ask.

"Because he's dead."

At that moment, as if on cue, two morticians emerge from the Science Building, carrying Dr Blaine's body on a stretcher. His corpse might be covered by a blanket, but somehow you know it's him, and you shiver, as if someone just walked over your grave.

"So, what happens now?" you ask Detective Harden.

"To him? The body will be taken to St Mary's where a full autopsy will be carried out in due course to determine the cause of death." The detective hands the jotter back to you. "But if you mean regarding the notebook, not a lot. Keep it. I don't think it's going to be of much use to our inquiries at the moment."

He hesitates momentarily before handing you a small rectangle of card printed with his name and a telephone number.

"Here's where you can contact me if you need to."

You thank him and put [DETECTIVE HARDEN'S CARD] in a coat pocket. Take the SECRET: *The Detective.*

> If you have a [BLACK TALON], turn to 121.
> If not, turn to 140.

Your heart hammering against your ribs, you grip the window frame and, using a footstool to help you, climb out onto the roof. You take a minute to steady yourself, trying not to look at the drop to the gravel path that yawns before you, and fix your eyes on the roof ridge instead. Using the projecting dormer window and a drainpipe to aid you, you make your careful ascent.

Making it to the top you are relieved to find the ridge itself is two feet wide and flat. You are less relieved when you see what awaits you there. It is like something out of a nightmare, and you can barely bring yourself to look at it. The thing is vaguely human in form, but its body appears to be emaciated, its skin black and rubbery. However, in other ways the entity is entirely inhuman. A long, barbed tail whips the air behind it while a pair of membranous wings protrude from its shoulder blades. Two horns sprouting from its head have turned inward, but worst of all is its face: it doesn't have one. Lose -1 SANITY.

Before you can make sense of what you are seeing, the creature emits an acidic hiss – even though you can see no mouth capable of making such a sound – and launches itself at you, elongated claws outstretched.

This is going to be a challenging fight, as it is going to be hard to hold your nerve in the face of the monstrosity's attack! You may spend **1 RESOURCES** at the start of each round to add 2 to your total for that round – if you have the **RESOURCES** to spend, that is.

Round one: roll two dice and add your **COMBAT** and your **WILLPOWER**. If you have the {SECRET RITES} Ability, add 1. If the total is 12 or more, you win the first round.

Round two: roll two dice and add your **COMBAT** and your **WILLPOWER**. If you have the {SECRET RITES} Ability, add 1. If you won the first round, add 2. If your total is 13 or more, you win the second round.

> If you won the second round, turn to **132**.
> If you lost the second round, turn to **235**.

Incredibly, you manage to get the better of the beast. When it realizes you are not going to be the easy kill it thought you were going to be, it flies off into the night on eerily silent wings. Take **+1 COMBAT** and **+1 WILLPOWER**.

> Turn to **11**.

You enter unobserved and take cover behind a potted tree fern. You take in the half-in-shadow faces of those around you, including Dr Blaine, and see that your companion has his flinty gaze fixed on the high priestess of the cult, Professor Nidus. The atmosphere inside the curious conservatory is electric. It crackles with potential that makes you feel as if a million ants are crawling under your skin.

"What do we do now?" you whisper, the droning chant of the cultists meaning that they remain deaf to what you are saying.

"We wait," Dr Blaine replies, without taking his eyes from Professor Nidus. "Now be quiet."

You feel tense. What is he waiting for? If the devotees of the Lord of Swarms need to be stopped, then surely their ritual needs to be brought to an end as quickly as is humanly possible.

What do you think it best to do?

> Do as Dr Blaine commands and wait: turn to **256**.
> Take matters into your own hands and do something to interrupt the ritual: turn to **24**.

Taking the [CEREMONIAL DAGGER] in hand once more, you test its weight and then, putting all your strength into your arm, hurl it at the sorcerer. The blade spins through the air and strikes Dr Blaine between the shoulder blades and stays there.

While you doubt such a blow itself is a mortal wound, Nyarlathotep's chosen doubles up in agony as what looks like tendrils of a shadowy substance uncoil from around where the knife has penetrated his flesh.

Just as you used the artifact to cut through the wards of protection that had been cast upon Abaddan House, so the Blade of Ark'at is having a similar effect on the sorcerous power that flows through Dr Blaine's veins. He drops to the ground, a rictus of pain on his face, and before your eyes he starts to transform, his skin turning gray and becoming even more lined, as if time is finally catching up with him.

Having dealt Dr Blaine what would appear to be a mortal wound after all, what do you want to do now?

Flee Abaddan House as fast as you can: turn to **300**. Turn your attention to the two rival factions who are even now engaged in all-out war with each other: turn to **249**.

There are simply too many of them, and despite putting up a valiant defense, and Dr Blaine bringing to bear all manner of esoteric energies against them, eventually the Cult of Assimilation have the two of you in their clutches. Almost insensible from the beating you have received, you are in no condition to resist as half a dozen of the black-robed villains drag you and Dr Blaine to the raised plinth in the center of the space.

Professor Nidus regards you now, a look of triumph on her pinched face. She does not falter in her chanting. In fact, if anything, she seems to do so with even greater gusto, urging the throng to raise the volume of their own voices. Bloated bluebottles and stick-thin mosquitoes whirl about you through the air as you are hauled up the steps closer to the high priestess. However, between you are her stands the strange terracotta vessel.

The ritual reaches its climax, the voices of the cult raised in jubilation. Professor Nidus throws her hands into the air and from the mouth of clay pot pours a torrent of huge black insects. They look like a grotesque cross between a scarab beetle and a tarantula hawk. The creatures quickly fill the conservatory, blackening the air and blocking your view of what is happening upon the plinth. In mere moments hundreds have emerged from the impossible vessel, then thousands, then tens of thousands. The screaming begins.

You hear Dr Blaine give voice to an exclamation of bitter regret before his words are drowned out by the buzzing voice of the swarm.

Ezel-zen-rezl is not one being but a gestalt entity, an incomprehensibly huge hive mind made up of billions of the creatures the Cult of Assimilation calls trylogogs. A portion of this impossible swarm emerges now, using the cicada vessel as a way into the world, like some Biblical plague of locusts. And like locusts, the trylogogs start to scour the conservatory of all organic matter, intending to ultimately make it part of Ezel-zen-rezl. That includes all the exotic plants growing in the conservatory, every single one of the cultists trapped within, including Professor Nidus, and Dr Blaine.

And you.

The End.

The globe is clearly quite old but has been carefully preserved. You can't help giving it a spin within its cradle. As it slows to a stop, you hear a soft click. It doesn't open to reveal a concealed drinks trolley, however. Instead, part of the wall covered with the map of the world hinges open, revealing only blackness beyond. You have found a secret door!

If you want to see where the door leads, turn to **136**. If you would prefer to leave the room before... something... enters through the secret door, turn to **151**.

As you struggle to keep your "hostage" from hurting you, the others pile in. Both you and Dr Blaine are overwhelmed by sheer force of numbers and soon find yourselves in the clutches of the cultists. Lose - **1 HEALTH.**

You struggle against the iron grip of the twisted men and women but there are too many of them and, in the end, you have to admit that you are now their prisoner. It would appear that all is lost.

Make a fate test. Roll one die, and if you have the Weakness **{CURSED}**, add 1.

If the result is equal to or lower than the current **DOOM** level, turn to **232.**
If not, turn to **177.**

Surely the best way to disrupt the ritual is to create a little chaos within the conservatory, but how are you going to do that? Desperately, you take in your surroundings, hoping that they might provide you with the inspiration you need.

Make an invention test. Roll one die and add your **INTELLECT**. You may spend 1 **CLUE** to roll two dice and pick the highest. What's the result?

> Total of 8 or more: turn to **129**.
> 7 or less: turn to **149**.

The dead man's chest suddenly convulses before collapsing completely, and from within his clothes emerges a swarm of the hideous bugs. Their iridescent wings a flickering blur, a droning hum fills the morgue as the horde take to the air.

What do you want to do?

> Flee: turn to **130**.
> Prepare to defend yourself, as best you can: turn to **220**.
> Try something else: turn to **240**.

111

As you watch Dr Waugh descend from the night sky astride his unnatural steed, you realize there are dozens of people crawling over the glass panels of the conservatory roof!

Professor Nidus's shrieking is suddenly silenced by the simultaneous shattering of a hundred panes of glass, and the astrophysicist's followers drop into the conservatory, heedless of their own safety.

"Members of the Cult of the Empty Sky," Dr Blaine tells you, raising his voice to be heard over the clamor that echoes from the walls of the breached conservatory. "They worship Silenus, 'The Empty Sky.' They are nihilists and believe there is no point to anything, and therefore embrace death as the only logical answer. Watch out for them, for they fear nothing, least of all their own end."

You do not ask Dr Blaine how he knows so much about the new arrivals and instead consider what to do next. But as you are trapped in the loop of your own desperate thoughts, one of the nihilistic stargazers throws himself at you, unaware or uncaring of the fact that you are nothing to do with the Cult of the Swarm God.

How do you want to defend yourself?

With the Blade of Ark'at: turn to **143**.
With whatever other weapons you have available: turn to **160**.

"No," you say firmly, "I won't help you. How do I know you don't have dark designs of your own linked to the prophecy?"

Dr Blaine's face darkens. It seems to you that the lights in the diner dim in response. "Professor Nidus is the head of the Arkham branch of the Cult of Assimilation." His tone is icily cold. "They are dangerous fanatics who worship Ezel-zen-rezl, the Lord of Swarms. The Ezel-zen-rezl hive seeks to assimilate all organic life into itself and the Cult of Assimilation is working for it to achieve that very goal. The weak-minded fools believe assimilation into the swarm to be an honor. Can you imagine?"

Your skin crawls at the thought of thousands of insect bodies scuttling all over you.

"Nidus has acquired the means to unleash the swarm upon the world and they will do so this very night if we don't stop them. So, what do you say now? Will you assist me in this task?"

It might be that the old adage "the enemy of my enemy is my friend" applies in this instance, but you have seen enough yourself to believe that Dr Blaine speaks the truth, and so to deny him your help could doom all of Arkham. You have no choice but to agree to help him.

Take +**1 CLUE** and +**1 INTELLECT**, but -**1 WILLPOWER**.

Turn to **69**.

113

Unbelievably, in the face of your stalwart defense, the ethereal entities retreat, rising out of reach on their nebulous wings, their beak-like mouths opening in silent shrieks of fear and frustration.

You decide it is time to leave Crane Hill yourself.

Take **+1 COMBAT** and turn to **140**.

114

The pinboard is covered with all sorts of pictures, photographs, maps, and newspaper clippings. The pictures grab your attention first. They are drawings of all manner of curious-looking creatures that appear like they would be the subject of folklore studies rather than zoology. However, there are numerous artists' impressions of what appears to be a curious egg, and if the figures drawn beside them are anything to go by, it is gigantic, many times the height of a man. Take the SECRET: *A Curate's Egg.*

The photographs all seem to have been taken in a jungle somewhere and feature a party of explorers. Among them is a much younger version of the man whose body is currently keeping you company in Dr Blaine's office. The various newspaper articles all appear to relate to reports of unsubstantiated witness accounts of curious phenomena in and around Arkham.

Most prominent among the maps is one of the town. A selection of places have been circled using a red wax crayon, but most of them show no indication of what might be there. There are two circled locations, however, that pinpoint specific buildings. One is a house in French Hill district, and the other is Miskatonic University itself, where you are right now. Take **+1 CLUE**.

A gust of wind from the open window sets the papers pinned to the board rustling, and you worry why it is unlatched at all.

Where do you want to look next in your quest for answers?

> The desk? Turn to **154**.
> The large bookcase? Turn to **175**.
> Through the open window? Turn to **134**.
> Somewhere other than Dr Blaine's study? Turn to **215**.

115

Just being within the walls of the grim gothic edifice could make a person feel ill, you think, as you explore the wards and corridors of St Mary's Hospital. There is certainly an unhealthy air about the place, and something more than the general miasma of illness you would expect. Take the SECRET: *Location Five*.

While you are sure there are myriad secrets hidden behind its whitewashed walls, you can discover no further leads that might help you in your quest for answers. In the end you are forced to admit defeat and look elsewhere.

> Take -1 WILLPOWER and +2 DOOM – but you may spend 1 CLUE or 1 RESOURCES to reduce the DOOM penalty by 1; or spend 2 CLUES or 2 RESOURCES to avoid adding any DOOM. Then turn to 140.

116

Looking both ways along the corridor and listening intently for any sound that would indicate someone is nearby, confident at last that you are alone, you pick up an ashtray stand and strike the glass panel. It shatters with a crystalline sharpness, and you freeze, fearful that someone must have heard and will come to investigate at any moment.

When they don't, you reach through, in the hope that you

can unlock the door from the inside. Unfortunately, there is no catch on the inside. The door can only be unlocked using the appropriate key.

Thinking you hear a sound behind you, you whip your hand back through but manage to slice your arm on a jagged piece of broken glass in the process. You give a sharp intake of breath and wince as you clamp your other hand over the wound. Not only it is painful, but it also requires you to improvise a bandage, and it will make it harder to use the injured arm.

Lose - **1 HEALTH** and - **1 COMBAT**.

You hear another sound, louder this time, a crash. Instinctively, you set off in the direction of the noise and soon find yourself standing inside the observatory proper. A grand, iron-wrought staircase leads up to the platform on which stands the impressive telescope. There is a distinct chill in the air as the dome is partially open so that the night sky can be viewed through the telescope.

Turn to **170**.

116

"It must be fascinating work," you say, "studying creatures that are so alien to ourselves."

"You have no idea," the entomologist mutters under his breath.

"Is that a titan beetle?" you ask, pointing at one of the glass jars on a shelf above the workbench.

"Yes. *Titanus giganteus.*"

"They're quite rare, aren't they?"

"Yes," Dr Christopher confirms. His eyes move to the cloth again. "But not as rare as this."

"And what might that be?"

The doctor hesitates for a moment, as if fearing someone might step into his office unannounced and interrupt the two of you at any moment. Then, "Take a look for yourself," he says, his voice low but unable to hide the sudden twinkle that appears in his eye. With that, he pulls the cloth away.

The sight of what lies on the dissecting board beneath makes you take an involuntary step backward, even though the thing is clearly dead. It looks like some sort of gigantic hornet, but several times larger than any you have even heard of, and its chitinous carapace is an oily black. It is secured to the board by several large pins. Its stained glass wings fully extended to a span of two feet. A sting, like a steel needle, projects from a bulbous abdomen and looks like it could cause a nasty wound, aside from whatever toxin must be stored within its poison sacs.

"What on Earth is that?" you ask, not daring to take your eyes off the insect for a second, as if expecting it to suddenly come to twitching life and tear free of the dissecting board.

"That is what I am trying to find out," says Dr Christopher.

Each new revelation merely serves to deepen the mystery.

You are desperate to learn more. You tell the entomologist as much.

"Professor Nidus has an office on the second floor, beyond the Kafka collection," he tells you as you turn to the door. "But if she's not there, she lives in a grand house in French Hill."

Thanking Dr Christopher for his help you leave his office, pulling the door shut on your way out. Take **+ 1 CLUE**.

> If you want to make your way to Professor Nidus's office, turn to **298**.
> If you would prefer to leave the Science Building and pursue your investigations elsewhere, turn to **140**.

Is there somewhere in particular that you would like more information on? If so, turn the letters of the location's two-word name into numbers, using the code A=1, B=2... Z=26, add them up, multiply the result by two, and then turn to the same section as the total.

If the section you turn to makes no sense, or if you can't think of a place to inquire about, Carol cannot help you.

> You will have to leave the library and look elsewhere for clues: turn to **140**.
> If you want to spend **1 CLUE** to help you solve the puzzle, turn to **265**.

119

"No!" you snap back, unsettled by the woman's strange behavior. "I don't want to hear what you have to say. Leave me alone!"

"Very well," she grumbles. "Remain in the darkness of your ignorance then. But don't say you weren't warned."

Turn to **219**.

120

You have received no clear indication that anyone has seen you, but you can't shake the feeling that someone, or some*thing*, is watching you from behind the dark windows of the house. Although the shadows that smother the grounds surrounding the house unnerve you as well – your imagination populating them with all manner of hidden horrors – you nevertheless decide to strike out across the lawns, away from the lamp-lit porch, and search for an alternative way in.

Skirting the building, you return to the gravel path that surrounds the mansion as the west wing comes into view. One of the windows at the end of the house appears to be ajar. Creeping up to it, you peer inside and see a hallway of walnut wood paneling, heavy cerise drapes, and large potted plants on turned wooden stands.

> If you want to enter the house through the open window, turn to **148**.
> If you want to change your mind and return to the front door, turn to **18**.

You saw the body and you were attacked by whatever it was that attempted to flee the scene of the crime, and which you presume attacked Dr Blaine. But you weren't certain the old man was dead… there definitely weren't any obvious signs of injury on his body. Something about this whole situation just doesn't quite ring true.

You don't feel you can trust anything anyone tells you, especially people in positions of power. Your only confidence comes from trusting what you witness for yourself. Even then you are not sure you can entirely believe what you have seen with your own eyes this evening.

> If you want to follow as the body makes the journey to St Mary's Hospital, turn to **279**.
> If not, turn to **140**.

122

You have had an exhausting evening and are glad to be back within the welcoming embrace of Velma's Diner. While you are there you have a cup of strong coffee and a slice of apple pie. Take the SECRET: *Location One*.

But returning to this place does not provide you with any more answers regarding the fate of the mysterious Dr Blaine, so it is time to look somewhere else.

Take + **1 HEALTH** and + **1 DOOM**.

> Turn to **140**.

123

Although the proprietor and the clientele of Ye Olde Magick Shoppe keep unusual hours, you find the store shut up for the night. No amount of knocking on the door makes any difference; Miriam Beecher clearly does not want to be disturbed on this night of all nights. You are going to have to look elsewhere for answers.

Take the SECRET: *Location Two*. Spend either **1 CLUE** or **1 RESOURCES** or take + **1 DOOM**.

> Turn to **140**.

Happy that you are part of the cult, the heads in question return their attention to Professor Nidus and the curious vessel standing on the stone table in front of her. Your disguise worked. That was good thinking. Take **+1 INTELLECT.**

Leaning in close to Dr Blaine you whisper, "What do we do now?"

"We wait," he replies, his eyes fixed on Professor Nidus too. "Now, be quiet."

You feel tense. What is he waiting for? If the worshippers of Ezel-zen-rezl need to be stopped, then surely their ritual needs to be brought to an end as quickly as is humanly possible.

What do you think it best to do?

> Do as Dr Blaine commands and wait: turn to **256**.
> Take matters into your own hands and do something to interrupt the ritual: turn to **24.**

This mystery appears to be focused around goings-on at Miskatonic University, particularly the enmity between Dr Blaine and Professor Nidus that you witnessed boil over at the diner. Therefore, it makes sense to you to find out what you can about Professor Nidus, to get a better idea of what was the source of their conflict, and therefore by extension, what actually happened to Dr Blaine.

At this late hour, this corner of the campus is quiet, and you do not see anyone about as you make your way to the Science Building. Inside, dull yellow bulbs give the corridor walls a nicotine stain. Using the information painted on polished walnut signboards, you find yourself entering the Entomology Department, where Professor Nidus teaches.

Behind the empty receptionist's desk, a board displaying the names of the academics who work in the department states whether they are "IN" or "OUT." According to the name board, Professor Nidus, like the rest of her colleagues, is "OUT." In fact, there is only one faculty member whose status is currently "IN," and that is one Dr Milan Christopher.

If you want to make your way to Professor Nidus's office, turn to **298**.

If you want to look in on Dr Milan Christopher, turn to **168**.

Clipped to the board is a piece of paper with a list of names scribbled on it in a barely legible hand. You see that the name *Dr D. Blaine* has been added at the bottom and beside it, in much clearer handwriting has been written #78.

One other name stands out, not because it is written particularly clearly, but because it has been crossed out. You can still see the number that had been allocated to it, however: #87. Make a note and take + **1 CLUE.**

Choosing something you haven't tried already, what do you want to do now?

Take a closer look at the pills: turn to **96.**
Enter the morgue: turn to **156.**

No matter how hard you try, in such a high stress situation as this, you cannot come up with a way to engineer the outcome you desire. Take - **1 INTELLECT.**

Two of the battling cultists barge into you and send you tumbling to the ground where you scrape your hands and knees on the unforgiving stone floor. Lose - **1 HEALTH**.

Time is running out, so you are going to have to try something else. But what's it to be?

Flee from this place as fast as you can: turn to **260**.

Attack Dr Blaine: turn to **77**.

Focus your attention on trying to stop the summoning of Ezel-zen-rezl: turn to **157**.

Concentrate on stopping the emergence of Silenus, the Empty Sky: turn to **185**.

Make the ultimate sacrifice in order to deny the schemes of the Outer Gods vying for power in this place: turn to **50**.

128

Fortunately, at this time of day, there are plenty of available cabs cruising the streets of Easttown. However, you are slightly taken aback when the face you are greeted by at the driver's window appears to be that of a beardless youth who can barely be old enough to drive.

"Where you heading?" he asks in a high-pitched voice.

The Checker carrying the woman is turning onto the main thoroughfare that leads south to the river.

"Follow that cab," you say as you open the door and take a seat.

Your initial assumption was correct. The Checker

crosses the river and then proceeds along Peabody Avenue. South of the river, the wharfs and warehouses give way to the colonial mansions of French Hill – crumbling piles kept secluded within their own far-reaching estates, hidden behind high fences and overgrown hedges, or ringed by private woodland.

However, you lose sight of the cab you are following when an ancient jalopy pulls out suddenly in front of your vehicle. The cabbie swears imaginatively and thumps the steering wheel as the rickety vehicle belches out a cloud of oily smoke and proceeds to chug along in front of you with no apparent sense of haste at all.

Despite continuing to cruise the streets of French Hill area for another twenty minutes, you see no sign of the Checker or its passenger. Take +1 **CLUE**.

"I'm sorry," your driver says, "but it looks like we've lost him. What do you want to do now? You want me to drop you off somewhere or take you back to Velma's?"

You only have one other lead you can follow.

"No," you reply. "Take me to Miskatonic University."

Turn to **21**.

129

Distracting the disciples and disrupting the ritual is only the first step, but surely it would be better for whatever you intend to do next if those present didn't find it so easy to see you.

Using whatever you have to hand, you target one of the lamps that illuminates the conservatory and let fly. There is a sharp *pop* as you score a direct hit, and gasps go up from some of those present. But by then you have already targeted another lightbulb, then another, and another.

> Take + 1 **INTELLECT** and turn to **13**.

130

The most sensible decision would appear to you to be to get out of the morgue as fast as you can, before the swarm sees you as a potential threat and attacks.

> If you have picked up a [TOE-TAG], turn to **214**.
> If not, turn to **266**.

131

The door is unlocked. Opening it, you step through into a room that is in utter darkness. The only light comes from the lamps in the corridor behind you. As you are searching for a light switch, or even a candle and tinderbox, with a sudden bang the door slams shut, plunging you into total darkness.

You turn instinctively and grab for the door handle, but before you can give it a twist, you hear the click of a key turning in the lock. You have been locked in!

You feel a rising sense of panic within you and your heart rate quickens.

If you want to try to force the door, turn to **71**.

If you want to try to remain calm and search the room, hoping to find a light switch or an electric lamp you can turn on, turn to **91**.

132

During your struggle against the unearthly monstrosity, you somehow manage to snag one of its wings on a roof-spike that projects from the edge of the roof where the ridge runs out. The horror gives another sharp hiss as it recoils in pain and, as a direct result, loses its balance.

Instinctively, it hops from the roof into the air. Normally its wings, and the ability to fly, would save it, but the spike has clearly done more damage than either you or the beast realized. The torn pinion cannot support it and, as it starts to fall, its other wing tangles within the ragged flaps of torn membrane.

The creature plummets over thirty feet to the ground. Tentatively, you crawl to the end of the roof ridge and peer over. You can just make out the contorted form of the creature, lying motionless on the ground at the foot of the Science Building. Embedded between the roof tiles next to you, where it scrabbled at the roof to save itself, it has left behind a single [BLACK TALON]. Take +1 COMBAT and the Ability {AGILE}.

Your heart racing from your improbable encounter with the faceless creature, as your mind tries to process what you have witnessed, you take in your surroundings and consider your situation. Further along the ridge, iron-grilled steps lead to a fire escape, which would lead you back down to the ground. Alternatively, you could return the way you came and re-enter the seemingly dead academic's study.

What's it to be?

> If you want to descend the fire escape, turn to **152**.
> If you want to climb back through the window into the study, turn to **277**.

133

No matter what you try, you are unable to beat back the smoky wraiths. After all, how can you harm something that has no physical body?

Consumed by terror, and not knowing what else to do, you give in to instinct and react as a prey animal would; you turn tail and flee. All thoughts of finding Dr Waugh are driven from your mind as fear takes over. You run from the Warren Observatory, hoping that whatever the wisp-winged things are that they do not see fit to pursue you, or that you can outrun them.

You decide it is time to leave Crane Hill yourself.

Lose - **1 SANITY** and turn to **140**.

Through the window you can see that night has almost fallen, the university buildings transformed into anonymous blocks of darkness that cut rectangles and triangles out of the indigo sky. But not every silhouette outlined against the horizon is a regular shape. There is something out there, you are sure of it. Something that's alive.

If you want to climb out of the window onto the sloping roof to investigate, turn to **102**.
If you would prefer to stay exactly where you are, turn to **215**.

135

Following the directions the receptionist gives you, you soon find your way to the corridor where Dr Waugh's office is located. The solid wooden door has a pane of frosted glass set within it. You knock on the door but hear nothing from the other side. You try again. Still no response.

Boldly, you take hold of the handle and try to open the door, but it is locked. You try again, rattling the handle, but the door does not move an inch. The building is new and is solidly built. There hasn't been time for the doors to warp and shift within their frames.

If you are determined to enter Dr Waugh's office, you will have to try a different approach. You did not see anybody else on the way here and the other office doors are closed. In fact, an oppressive hush holds dominion here.

> If you want to break the glass panel in the door to gain entry to the office, turn to **116**.
> If you think it unwise to attempt a break in, turn to **145**.

136

Cautiously, you push the door open further and step through. You have not gone far into the darkness when you begin to notice a dull green glow. At the end of only a short passageway you find yourself in a small room. The walls are covered with ornate wallpaper, the pattern on it making you think of tessellating flies.

There is nothing in the room apart from a short plinth on top of which, resting on a piece of black velvet, is what is quite clearly a knife of some kind. It puts you in mind of a [CEREMONIAL DAGGER]. However, you are not entirely sure what it is made of. In this strange emerald light, you're not sure if it's metal. You're not even sure if the blade is made of some kind of stone. It almost looks organic – a material like horn or even shell.

For the blade to have been hidden like this, you are sure it is of immense importance, if not actually some artifact of great power. All the evidence would also suggest that Professor Nidus's father stole the blade in the first place.

You take the object in hand and immediately feel a renewed confidence, convinced that whatever travails still await you, you will be able to more effectively overcome them armed with the curious knife. It is ultimately for that reason you decide to take it with you. After all, if you don't survive the night, maybe the town of Arkham won't either. Add the [CEREMONIAL DAGGER] to your Character Sheet.

Your heart racing at having committed the crime of theft, you do not feel like hanging about any longer. Leaving the secret room, you exit the map room and return to the corridor beyond.

Take the SECRET: *Is This a Dagger I See Before Me?*

Turn to **151**.

The Orne Library is hardly inviting, comprising three floors of weathered gray granite, watched over by gargoyles that stand guard above arched windows, their savage snarls locked in stone for all eternity. Take the SECRET: *Location Six.*

Fortunately for you, the library is open late so that students attending Miskatonic University can study into the night, after their lectures and seminars have finished for the day. However, it is also home to some 400,000 books, and you could spend many hours, if not days, searching for something that could help you in your quest, so you warily approach the main desk. Standing behind it is an elderly librarian, her hair a mass of gray curls.

"Good evening," she says. "My name is Carol. Is there anything I can help you with?"

If you have the Weakness {**PARANOID**}, turn to **65**.
If not, turn to **118**.

As you keep your "hostage" from breaking free of your grasp, the other cultists pile in. If you are going to stop yourself being overwhelmed by the Disciples of the Swarm, you are going to have to let your captive go anyway, just so you can defend yourself.

You may spend **1 RESOURCES** at the start of each round to add 2 to your total for that round.

Round one: roll two dice and add your **COMBAT**. If the total is 17 or more, you win the first round.

Round two: roll two dice and add your **COMBAT**. If you won the first round, add 2. If your total is 18 or more, you win the second round. If you lose the second round, lose **-1 HEALTH**.

> If you won the second round, turn to **269**.
> If you lost the second round, turn to **257**.

Just being within the walls of the grim gothic edifice could make a person feel ill, you think as you explore the wards and corridors of Saint Mary's Hospital. There is certainly an unhealthy air about the place, and something more than the general miasma of illness you would expect. Take the SECRET: *Location Five.*

While you are sure there are myriad secrets hidden behind its whitewashed walls, you can discover no more leads that might help you in your quest for answers. In the end you are forced to admit defeat and look elsewhere.

> Take -1 **WILLPOWER** and +2 **DOOM** – but you may spend 1 **CLUE** or 1 **RESOURCES** to reduce the **DOOM** penalty by 1; or spend 2 **CLUES** or 2 **RESOURCES** to avoid adding any **DOOM**. Now turn to **140**.

140

There is clearly more to this mystery than just the strange fate met by Dr Blaine, but where do you want to go next in search of answers?

If you know of a suitable location, ignoring the definite article, the placename will be made up of two words. For example, if you wanted to visit "The City Hall" you would just use the words *City* and *Hall*. Turn the letters of the location into numbers, using the code A=1, B=2... Z=26, add the numbers together, and then turn to the same section as the total.

A	B	C	D	E	F	G	H	I	J
1	2	3	4	5	6	7	8	9	10

K	L	M	N	O	P	Q	R	S	T
11	12	13	14	15	16	17	18	19	20

U	V	W	X	Y	Z
21	22	23	24	25	26

If the section makes no sense, you have either made a mistake in your calculations or that particular place cannot be visited. If there is somewhere else you know of that you could try, repeat the process outlined above.

If you end up at a dead end, turn to **3**.

You leave Ye Olde Magick Shoppe, the bell jangling cheerily as you step over the threshold and back into the chilly night. However, you cannot shake the chill that has already permeated your bones since entering the shop. Spend **1 RESOURCES** or lose - **1 WILLPOWER**.

You consider the words written on the flyleaf of the jotter. Perhaps it would make more sense to head for Miskatonic University instead.

Turn to **21**.

"Something tells me you already know I do," you say, leaving the [CEREMONIAL DAGGER] where it is, hidden inside your coat.

"I want to see it," Dr Blaine says, the excitement clear in his voice. "Show it to me."

"Before I do, why don't you tell me why it is so important to you?"

The academic regards you for a moment, as a cat might regard a cornered mouse. "It is the Blade of Ark'at," he says, evidently having made up his mind to be open with you.

"And what is *that*?"

"As I am sure you have already worked out, it is an artifact of great power," he declares.

"But what do you want with it?" you ask, putting a hand on the blade within your coat. You suspect that the real answer isn't that he wants to take it for safekeeping within Miskatonic University's collection of curios and esoteric texts.

"Very well. Due to the path I have taken in life and promises I have made, I am bound by certain restrictions that have prevented me from entering Abaddan House. But enter the house I must, if I am to prevent the imminent apocalypse that faces us now, and the blade is the key that will permit me entrance."

Apocalypse? Dr Blaine doesn't mince his words. And you are sure he is serious too, or at least fervently believes what he is telling you.

Before you go any further, you demand that he tells you what is going on.

"You decoded my notebook, didn't you? Do you not recall the prophecy? A god will rise in Arkham? Professor Nidus is working to make it her god that claims dominion. I need your help to stop her."

What do you want to do?

> If you agree to help Dr Blaine thwart Professor Nidus's plans, turn to **88**.
> If you refuse, **112**.

Seeing you brandishing the blade before you, the follower of Silenus stumbles to a halt. What can it be about the artifact that has caused the nihilist to pause when you thought the worshippers of Silenus feared nothing?

"Strike! Strike now!" Dr Blaine shouts. You can feel something underneath his words – a power unchecked running through the command.

Make a strength of will test. Roll one die and add your **WILLPOWER**. If you have the {**SORCERY**} Ability, add 2 to the result. What is the total?

> 9 or more: turn to **217**.
> 8 or less: turn to **237**.

You suddenly find yourselves the focus of the attention of a half-dozen cultists. You stand out like a sore thumb, thanks to the fact that you are not wearing the same black robes that everyone else present has on. While the rest of the room continues to chant the words of the unholy rite, those cultists who have spotted you break ranks and move toward you, as if they intend to seize you or eject you from the conservatory.

How will you respond?

If you think you have something that you could use to defend yourself, turn to **48**.

If you want to prepare to fight the cultists, turn to **138**.

If you want to grab one of the cultists and take them hostage, turn to **42**.

145

Locked doors usually need a key to open them. If you happen to come across such an item while you are exploring the Warren Observatory, deduct the number stamped on the key from the section you are on at the time and then turn to this new section. But clearly, you have other investigating to do at the moment.

> Turn to **97**.

146

Incredibly, the impossible winged beast crashes down on top of the stone dais, sending Professor Nidus's precious clay pot crashing to the ground where it shatters into a million terracotta shards. In her rage and frustration, she throws herself at Dr Waugh, who is struggling to extricate himself, half-trapped as he is under his dying steed. Take **+1 COMBAT**.

Now's your chance! With the leader of Cult of the Empty Sky and the herald of Silenus dealt with, what do you want to do?

> Flee from this place: turn to **260**.
> Attack Dr Blaine: turn to **77**.
> Turn your attention to overpowering those of the Cult of the Assimilation who remain: turn to **249**.

"They're ugly things, aren't they?" you say, nodding at the jars of preserved specimens.

Dr Christopher regards you with a puzzled expression on his face. "I'm sorry?"

"Insects," you say. "Creepy crawlies."

"Oh no!" the entomologist says disparagingly. "There is great beauty within the insect world, if one knows where to look. After all, they are evolution's ultimate accomplishment. What was it you said you wanted with Professor Nidus?"

"I didn't," you reply. "It's all right. I had best be going anyway."

With that, you leave Dr Christopher's office of your own volition.

Add the Weakness {PARANOID} to your Character Sheet, if you don't already have it.

You cannot shake the creeping sense of unease that has come over you and that seems to intensify the longer you remain within the Science Building. Nonetheless, you have yet to track down the mysterious Professor Nidus.

What do you want to do now?

To make your way to Professor Nidus's office, turn to **298**.

To leave the Science Building and pursue your investigations elsewhere, turn to **140**.

Unlatching the window, you open it fully and, putting a foot on a piece of projecting stonework and your hands on the window frame, you push yourself up onto the windowsill and climb inside.

However, as you do so, you catch your leg on a rusty nail that is protruding from the warped wood of the frame. You wince in pain but as you pull yourself free, you tumble through the window onto the carpeted floor on the other side, the rusty metal tearing the skin from your knee to your ankle. Lose -1 HEALTH.

Stealing a napkin from under one of the potted plants, you press on the wound with the cloth until you have managed to stem the bleeding. Fortunately, no one appears to have been alerted to your presence by your ungainly entrance, but the lit lamps would suggest that there is someone at home.

With the window at your back, you see one door further along the corridor to your left and another to the right. Beyond that, an archway beckons you to explore the rest of the house that lies beyond the west wing.

Where do you want to look first?

To try the door to your left, turn to **55**.
To try the door to your right, turn to **131**.
To head deeper into the house beyond the arch, turn to **194**.

It's no good, you can't come up with an appropriate plan quickly enough. And now the time for desperate last minute plans has passed.

Turn to **256**.

Despite the taxing travails you have suffered this night, much needed adrenaline gives your body the kick it needs, and you flee from Abaddan House, the cries of the battling cultists and the droning voice of the swarm fading into the distance.

But as you retrace the route you took to get here and find yourself outside, swaddled by the cold night air once more, something unbelievable and world-warping occurs. As you continue to flee through the grounds, you feel tremors under your feet and a sudden drop in air pressure, all of which is accompanied by the howling of a hurricane.

Risking no more than a glance over your shoulder, in that moment you witness what is happening to the house. The mansion appears to be collapsing. Impossible geometries take hold of the building as it begins to fold in on itself, brick walls bending, pitched roofs buckling, and windows shattering in their frames, as those same apertures are crushed shut.

You do not stop running, but increase your effort, panic driving you to exhaustion. Moonlight chases you as the eclipse passes and you look to the sky to see the moon has returned, the hole in the sky and the entity that lurked beyond it, both having vanished. Fatigued, your legs and lungs burning, you stumble to a halt and gaze across the moonlit estate. But of Abaddan House there is no sign. There is not even a footprint on the ground where it previously stood, no sign of a basement or wine cellar. Nothing at all but a sweep of untouched turf. It is as if the house never existed at all. In fact, your memories of the place are already starting to evaporate.

You have a resolution of sorts – Arkham is safe, and the Outer Gods remain trapped wherever it is that they wait for their chance to rise – but what happened to the Cult of the Empty Sky? And what about Dr Blaine? Is he still alive out there, somewhere?

It is strange to think that you encountered the so-called zoologist for the first time only a matter of hours ago, back at Velma's Diner. You suddenly feel the need to be surrounded by the comfort of the diner once more and so set off for Easttown. High over Arkham, tentacle-like tendrils of black cloud crawl across the heavens.

SECRET: *Live to Fight Another Day.*

Final score: 2 stars.

The End.

151

Your attention is suddenly grabbed by a sharp hum and turning your head you see two enormous insects buzzing toward you, their glass-like, iridescent wings a flickering blur. Their chitinous carapaces appear to have an oily sheen in the cool yellow glow that suffuses this part of the house. They look like an amalgamation of the most terrifying elements of a scarab beetle and a tarantula hawk.

You instinctively start to back away from the horror-hornets, as you consider your routes of escape and other options.

What do you want to do?

Stand your ground and prepare to battle the monstrous insects: turn to **205**.

Flee from Abaddan House without a second thought: turn to **166**.

152

You descend the black metal staircase at a stumbling run, holding onto the rail the whole way down. Upon reaching the bottom, you find yourself inexorably drawn to the spot where the nightmarish creature fell.

As you round the corner of the gray stone building – returning to the scene of the crime, as it were – you hear the crunch of tires on gravel and headlights sweep the end of the building, as a pair of police cars pull up outside the Science Building. As they do so, their headlamps momentarily illuminate the spot where the creature fell, and your heart jumps into your mouth. The monster has gone!

You immediately spin round, fearing the creature is waiting to ambush you from the shadows, but there is nothing there. However, four cops have bundled out of the cars and are making for the main entrance to the building you have just exited.

> If you want to approach the police, with the intention of talking to them, turn to **242**.
> If you would rather not draw attention to yourself and want to flee the scene, turn to **202**.

Drawing on your own esoteric powers, you focus on the curious ethereal entities and your desire to see them gone. As you do so, the wind begins to pick up, steadily increasing in strength, until it sweeps the smoky forms of your attackers away, leaving you to make good on your escape from the Warren Observatory. You do not stop running until you are at the bottom of Crane Hill once more.

> Turn to **140**.

You feel uncomfortable rummaging through the things on Dr Blaine's desk with his body spreadeagled in the chair beside you, but you need answers. But rather than answers, all you uncover are more questions. In one drawer you find a [LIGHTER], in another a loaded [PISTOL], and in a third, a half-empty bottle of [WHISKEY].

If you want to take any of these items, record them on your Character Sheet and take +1 RESOURCES for each item taken.

Turn to 215.

Astrophysics comes under the remit of the Department of Physics but is effectively its own department, with the offices of the faculty being found in the Warren Observatory.

Miskatonic University may be an ancient institution of longstanding, and much of it might seem like it is trapped in the nineteenth century, but it is still a growing organization. The Gerald Warren Astronomical Observatory is its latest addition. The building stands atop Crane Hill and looks not unlike a squat, art nouveau lighthouse, surmounted by a hemispherical dome. The observatory overlooks all of Arkham but those who use its great telescope and other measuring devices are not interested in enjoying the vista. Their attentions are focused on the heavens.

There are several lights on in the building and upon entering you are greeted by a receptionist sitting behind a solid mahogany counter. When she asks what business you have there, you ask her where you might find Dr Waugh.

"I believe he was scheduled to use the telescope this evening," the receptionist replies. "But if he's not there, you'll probably find him in his office."

Where do you want to start your search for Dr Waugh?

If you want to head to his office, turn to **135**.
If you would rather look for him in the observatory dome, turn **97**.

156

Stepping into the morgue, you pause, letting the door swing shut behind you. Clinical white tiles are lit by humming lamps, and the room smells strongly of bleach, rather than quietly decomposing bodies. It is, however, as cold as the tomb and as silent as the grave.

A dozen trolleys have been packed into the room in regimented rows, while the wall to your right is a bank of stainless steel hatches, six across and five high. You study the measurements intently.

Having come this far, you are curious to see if Dr Blaine's

body is really here, but you also feel deeply uneasy to be disturbing the sleep of the dead.

What do you want to do?

Look for Dr Blaine's body among those on the trolleys: turn to **186**.
Search for the academic in one of the refrigerated compartments that lie behind the gleaming metal hatches: turn to **226**.
Leave the morgue without disturbing the dead any more than you have already: turn to **246**.

It was the worshippers of Ezel-zen-rezl that you came here to stop and, as far as you are concerned, they still pose the greatest immediate threat. The Cult of the Empty Sky has only been forced to play its hand by the actions of Professor Nidus and her fellow bug-lovers, although you may have had a hand in that as well.

Shouldering your way between the battling cultists, you make for the raised stone platform. The Disciples of the Swarm have been forced to break off their chanting by the nihilistic stargazers' attack, but you can still hear a buzzing murmur that seems to repeat the name of their god over and over: "Ezel-zen-rezl. Ezel-zen-rezl! *Ezel-zen-rezl!*" Are you going mad?

But the buzzing sound isn't being made by the human servants of the Lord of Swarms – it is actually emitting from the droning of countless insects. The air is thick with them, and it seems to you that more are joining the locust-like mass all the time, teeming out of the mouth of the curious clay vessel.

Steeling yourself, you prepare to fight your way through the swarm to reach Professor Nidus and halt the summoning. You may spend 1 **RESOURCES** at the start of each round to add 2 to your total for that round.

Round one: roll two dice and add your **COMBAT**, but then deduct the current **DOOM** level. If you have the {AGILE} Ability, add 1. If you have the {SECRET RITES} Ability, add 1. If you have the Weakness {FEAR OF INSECTS} deduct 2. If the total is 15 or more, you win the first round.

Round two: roll two dice and add your **COMBAT**. If you have the {AGILE} Ability, add 1. If you have the {SECRET RITES} Ability, add 1. If you have the Weakness {FEAR OF INSECTS} deduct 2. If you won the first round, add 2. If your total is 16 or more, you win the second round.

Round three: roll two dice and add your **COMBAT**. If you have the {AGILE} Ability, add 1. If you have the {SECRET RITES} Ability, add 1. If you have the Weakness {FEAR OF INSECTS} deduct 2. If you won the second round, add 2. If your total is 16 or more, you win the third round.

If you won the third round, turn to **238**.
If you lost the third round, turn to **272**.

158

You make your way to the Easttown neighborhood and enter the Police Station, approaching the duty officer's desk. Take the SECRET: *Location Four*.

> If you have [INKY FINGERS], turn to **165**.
> If you have a [DETECTIVE HARDEN'S CARD], turn to **222**.
> If not, turn to **204**.

159

You find yourself transfixed by the woman's gaze. There is something there, moving in the pinpricks of darkness that are her pupils. And then she speaks.

"When the moon in darkness dies, then a new god shall arise. One from three shall claim the prize. One called from the burning pit, one that seeks the veil to split, the last the child, its egg forfeit."

The lilting chant sounds like a prophecy more than anything else. Take +1 CLUE and the SECRET: *Cracked*. But the look in her eyes and the subtle power behind her words unnerves you.

Make a fear test. Roll one die and add your WILLPOWER. You may spend 1 RESOURCES to roll two dice and pick the highest. If you have the Weakness {HAUNTED}, deduct 1. What's the result?

Total of 9 or more: turn to **179**.
8 or less: turn to **199**.

160

You have no choice but to defend yourself with whatever alternative means you have available to you. All around, the nihilistic servants of Silenus, the Empty Sky, are attacking the followers of Ezel-zen-rezl, the Lord of Swarms. In doing so, they have disrupted the ritual, preventing Professor Nidus from releasing their sinister god into the world, while their own mind-bending deity worries at the edges of the portal that yawns above the mansion where once the moon hung in the sky.

As a pair of Dr Waugh's followers charge toward you, you and Dr Blaine prepare to give as good as you get. You may spend 1 RESOURCES at the start of each round to add 2 to your total for that round.

Round one: roll two dice and add your **COMBAT**. If you have the {AGILE} Ability, add 1. If the total is 15 or more, you win the first round.

Round two: roll two dice and add your **COMBAT**. If you have the {AGILE} Ability, add 1. If you won the first round, add 2. If your total is 16 or more, you win the second round.

> If you won the second round, turn to **201**.
> If you lost the second round, turn to **184**.

No matter what it costs you, you must know what secret information is hidden within Dr Blaine's jotter.

"Very well, follow me," says the venerable Miriam Beecher and she leads you to a back room draped with moldering curtains and threadbare, gauzy drapes that make you feel like you have been transported into a down-at-heel fortune-teller's tent.

She sits down on one side of a small round table and invites you to take a seat opposite her. Take the SECRET: *The Fortune-Teller.*

"What I am about to share with you will change you forever," she says, placing [DR BLAINE'S NOTEBOOK] between you. "Once the door to knowledge has been opened, you will not be able to forget what you discover lies beyond – ever. Are you ready?"

You nod to confirm that you are, even as you feel the shadows at the corners of the room thicken and swell.

"Do these symbols appear at all familiar to you?" she asks, opening the notebook, seemingly at random.

If you have the {ANCIENT LANGUAGES} Ability, turn to **191**.
If not, turn to **231**.

162

Dr Blaine's smile falters for the first time since he joined you at your booth and the twinkle goes from his eyes. It is replaced by a glowering expression, and you feel a creeping coldness spreading throughout your body, turning your legs to lead and your stomach to ice.

"Oh dear, oh dear, oh dear," Dr Blaine says with crystal sharpness. "Such a disappointment. I had thought that once you found the notebook, the breadcrumbs I left would ultimately lead you to the prize."

What is he talking about?

"It wasn't as if you didn't have my help along the way. And yet here we are, at what would appear to be a dead end. Such a disappointment."

Before you are aware of what he is doing, the old man reaches across the table and grabs you by the hand. His touch burns with cold, and you instinctively try to cry out, but the utterance freezes in your throat.

"I cannot enter Abaddan House myself due to certain restrictions and covenants to which I am beholden. But a useful idiot, someone not bound by such restrictions, and yet still under my instruction – knowingly or otherwise – could."

The leaden chill continues to spread throughout your body, paralyzing you and forcing you to listen to Dr Blaine's confession.

"I couldn't risk trying to recruit you directly, of course. That would have raised your suspicions and then you might not have done what I needed you to do. But never mind, I will just have to find myself another unwitting accomplice."

With that, your body starts to shut down. In the face of the unremitting cold, the world retreats until it is only a pinprick of light amidst an oblivion of eternal darkness. And then even that tiny flicker and light is snuffed out.

The End.

Recalling the night horror that you battled on the roof of Miskatonic University, you take out its claw, intending to use it to strike down your erstwhile companion. But as you do so he fixes you with his burning gaze and something like a flicker of recognition passes across his face. And in that split second, you hurl the talon at him.

It spins through the air and strikes Dr Blaine, scoring a bloody line across his forehead.

"Impudent worm," the inhuman sorcerer spits. The blood that was only moments ago running freely from the gash in his head has already become a gloopy jelly that is being reabsorbed back into the wound. "You dare to challenge me?"

With that he points at you and one of the writhing shadow tentacles reaches for you. At the same time, you feel something cold and muscular wrap about your body and start to squeeze. There is nothing you can do as the sorcerer's shadow-limb pulls tighter and tighter. Bones break and blood spurts from ruptures in your flesh until you mercifully lose consciousness.

The End.

164

Leaving the book on the reading desk, you turn the pages and discover that it is full of aquatint plates of maps of the Americas. They are truly remarkable, overflowing with meticulous detail. But what is their relevance to the matter in hand, and why was the mysterious reader perusing them?

Take **+ 1 CLUE** and turn to **9**.

165

"I'm surprised to see you back here," the duty officer says. "If I was you, the minute I was out that door I would have kept walking and not looked back."

You explain that you want to help find Dr Blaine's killer.

"I told you, keep out of it," says the policeman. "Now clear off, and if I see you round here again, I'll put you back in the cells for the night for wasting police time."

You decide that there is nothing to be gained by pursuing your inquiries here, and so try to think of somewhere else you could look.

> Take +2 DOOM – though you may instead spend 1 CLUE or 1 RESOURCES to reduce the DOOM penalty by 1; or spend 2 CLUES or 2 RESOURCES to avoid adding any DOOM. Now turn to 140.

166

You turn tail and run, the hornet-like horrors powering after you on their hundred-beats-a-second wings. Ahead of you stands the front door to the house. Other than the unnatural insects, there is no other sign of life nearby, and certainly no obvious human presence, so unimpeded, you race for the way out.

Is it your imagination, or can you hear a furious buzzing

coming from behind the walnut paneling as you beat your hasty retreat through the house?

You run as fast as you can, but you cannot outrun the humming horrors. Their furious buzzing pursues you, coming ever closer, and you do your best to dodge out of their way of their jabbing stings and champing mandibles. But as you reach the door, in the moment that it takes you to yank it open, one of the critters manages to sting you.

It feels like a white-hot needle has been driven into your back and you half-fall at the threshold, the pain is so debilitating. Lose **-1 HEALTH.**

But then you are through the door and slamming it shut behind you again, trapping the creatures inside the house.

Turn to **264**.

By the time you decide to follow the other half of the arguing pair, the elderly gentleman has vanished from view as well. You make your way to the other end of the street as quickly as you can but can see no sign of him. He must have gotten a ride too.

You only have one other lead you can follow, and so set off for the other side of the river and Miskatonic University.

Turn to **227**.

168

It does not take you long to find Dr Christopher's rooms. According to the letters painted on his door, he is a Professor of Entomology. You are about to knock on the door when you hear a voice from the other side say, "It beggars belief!"

You assume the voice you can hear is that of Dr Christopher, but who is he speaking to? Is there someone else with him or is he talking to himself?

What do you want to do?

Knock on the door: turn to **188**.
Open the door and enter without knocking: turn to **169**.
Forget about Dr Christopher and go in search of Professor Nidus: turn to **298**.

169

You find yourself in a study that is filled with bookcases and freestanding shelves. Many of the shelves are packed with large glass jars, as well as books and bundles of paper. These clear containers are filled with a yellowy green liquid within which float all manner of curious specimens. The one thing they have in common is that they are all invertebrates – specifically of the taxonomic classification *insecta* – predominantly large beetles and spine-encrusted stick insects.

A large man stands in front of a workbench. He turns in surprise at your unexpected invasion of his privacy and for a moment you catch a glimpse of what he was examining. It looks like some sort of gigantic hornet with an oily black chitinous carapace. It is secured to a dissecting board by several large pins and its stained glass wings are fully extended to a span of two feet. A sting, like a steel needle, projects from a bulbous abdomen. Take + 1 CLUE.

"What is the meaning of this?" blusters the man, hastily dropping a muslin cloth over the specimen on the workbench. "May I *help* you?" he asks pointedly.

"I'm sorry," you apologize. "I was looking for Professor Nidus."

"Then you have come to the wrong place," he snaps, peering at you through a pair of half-moon spectacles. "As the sign on the door says, I am Dr Milan Christopher."

Dr Christopher is portly and sports a thick head of hair as well as a bushy beard. He is wearing blue overalls over his everyday clothes, and a red bowtie can be seen protruding from beneath his chin.

How will you respond?

Apologize and leave: turn to **208**.
Ask Dr Christopher about Professor Nidus: turn to **27**.

You don't know what it is that alerts you to the arrival of the ethereal visitors – perhaps it is a subtle change in air temperature, or the caress of an unexpected breeze on your skin. Or maybe it is something altogether more esoteric and unknowable than that. Nonetheless, whatever the reason, you look up and see something slip into the observatory through the open portion of the dome.

You struggle to make out a definitive form, but the impression you get is of a tendril of mist, or smoke, but independent of any obvious cloud or flame. As you are already looking in that direction, you catch sight of the second one more easily as it follows its partner into the observatory. This time you get the impression of wing-like appendages and a ridge of smoky spines running the length of what you might consider to be its back.

Your mind is at once telling you that what you are looking at is impossible and yet, at the same time, very real. And is it your own pervading sense of panic or are these ethereal entities really projecting an aura of malign intent?

What do you want to do?

Flee: turn to **32**.
Stand your ground: turn to **64**.
Try something else: turn to **93**.

For all its decaying old world charm and quaint window displays of horoscopes and tarot cards, Ye Olde Magick Shoppe of Arkham hides its true nature in plain sight. Most who find themselves walking past the store have no idea that it is a haven for those practitioners of the esoteric arts, for want of a better phrase.

Despite the late hour, Ye Olde Magick Shoppe is still open. As you enter the establishment a bell rings somewhere nearby and, hearing clicking footsteps, your attention is drawn to the gray-haired woman who is now standing behind the counter. Your gaze briefly flickers below to the counter's glass cabinets, which are full of esoteric curiosities. She wears a fashionable blouse and slacks, and a startling amount of antique jewelry. Her reputation precedes her: this is Miriam Beecher, the proprietor of the Magick Shoppe.

"Can I help you?" she asks pleasantly, whilst fixing you with the most piercing eyes.

In spite of any fears you might have about letting others know you are in possession of [DR BLAINE'S NOTEBOOK], you came here specifically to have someone help you decode its contents. Proffering Miriam the notebook you ask if she can help you translate what is written within. She pauses before taking it from you and then gives a few of the pages a cursory glance.

"As a rule of thumb, you should not meddle in things you do not understand," she says coldly, that piercing stare of hers unrelenting. "Especially here in Arkham."

You explain that it is too late for that, to which she replies, "Then there will be a price to pay."

"I have money," you tell her.

"I do not mean money," she says, and you feel a chill creep into your limbs as gooseflesh rises on your skin. "Do you still desire to discover the truth, no matter what it may cost you?"

Well, do you?

If you decide it is time to leave Ye Olde Magick Shoppe before you find yourself writing a check your body can't cash, turn to **141**.

If you are prepared to pay to gain insight into the contents of [DR BLAINE'S NOTEBOOK], **161**.

Currently, the greatest threat facing Arkham is the two portals by which eldritch entities wish to enter the world. And if that happens, the whole town could be wiped from the face of the earth. Therefore, the greatest weapon at your disposal are those two portals.

With a desperate plan in mind, you barge your way through the battling cultists and climb the steps to the top of the stone dais. Professor Nidus greets you with a look of abject surprise and a scream of anger. But before she can seize you with her talon-like fingers, you grab hold of the curious clay vessel that stands between you and point its open mouth at the portal that has opened in the sky over the eclipsed moon.

The high priestess of the Cult of Assimilation is furious that you have interrupted the ritual, but it appears that she has done enough, for in the next instant a torrent of huge black insects pours from the mouth of the vessel. They look like some nightmarish cross between a scarab beetle and a tarantula hawk. Their presence blackens the air around you and quickly blocks your view of the yawning portal.

The swarm becomes a focused column, like a beam of dark energy, that drives forward into the sky. Distances appear to warp and contract, until they mean nothing at all, and through the swarm you catch glimpses of colossal pincers attempting to sweep the bugs away, while myriad eyes bulge and roll in irritation, as forming and reforming mouths give voice to a yawning bellow of displeasure. Arms aching, you can hold the vessel no longer and let it drop to the floor, where it smashes into a thousand pieces. But it would appear that you too have done enough, for the swarm remains focused on attacking the abomination probing the portal far above.

It is time to leave. But between you and freedom there still stand battling cultists, swarming insects, and a maze of corridors and several closed doors.

Roll one die and add 1 if you have the {AGILE} Ability.

If the total is equal to or less than your HEALTH, turn to 250.
If the total is greater than your HEALTH, turn to 200.

173

The ritual being enacted within this place is intended to open a portal to somewhere else, a place where Ezel-zen-rezl waits to be summoned into the world. Focusing your mind, you concentrate on creating a magical barrier between you and the advancing cultists, much like the one Dr Blaine needed you to break so that he could enter Abaddan House. If you can hold them back, perhaps you then do something about halting the ritual altogether.

Turn to **13**.

174

Fire and alcohol don't mix well together, and fire and insects *really* don't mix.

Make an invention test. Roll two dice and add both your **INTELLECT** and your **COMBAT**. If you have the {**STUDIOUS**} Ability, add 1. What's the total?

14 or more: turn to **273**.
13 or less: turn to **254**.

175

The bookcase is a veritable treasure trove of esoteric literature. There is one ancient tome concerning *Alliances and Enmities Among the Outer Gods*, another called *The Gospel According to Ark'at*, and a third which is a guide to translating ancient languages.

If you want to take the languages guide, take the {ANCIENT LANGUAGES} Ability.

> Turn to **215**.

176

You are in the west wing of the house. The corridor you are now in has the feel of a lavish funeral parlor. Two doors lead off from the corridor, one to the left and the other to the right.

Which do you want to try?

> The door to the left: turn to **131**.
> The door to the right: turn to **55**.
> Neither: turn to **194**.

Despite your interruption, the rest of the cult do not falter in their chanting. Those who have you in their grasp drag the two of you against your will to the raised plinth in the center of the space.

Professor Nidus has her eyes fixed on you now, but she does not falter in her chanting either. In fact, if anything, she seems to do so with even greater gusto, urging the throng to raise the volume of their voices.

Bloated bluebottles and stick-thin mosquitoes whirl about you through the air as you are hauled up the steps toward the high priestess. However, between you stands the strange terracotta vessel. The ritual reaches its climax, the voices of the cult raised in jubilation. Professor Nidus throws her hands into the air and from the mouth of clay pot pours a torrent of huge black insects. They look like a panic-inducing cross between a scarab beetle and a tarantula hawk. The creatures quickly fill the conservatory, blackening the air and blocking your view of what is happening upon the plinth. In mere moments hundreds have emerged from the impossible vessel, then thousands, then tens of thousands. And the screaming begins.

Dr Blaine has mistimed things terribly. You hear him give voice to an exclamation of bitter regret before his words are drowned out by the buzzing voice of the swarm. Ezel-zen-rezl is not one being but a gestalt entity, an incomprehensibly huge hive mind made up of billions of the creatures the Cult of Assimilation calls trylogogs. A portion of this impossible swarm emerges now, using the cicada vessel as a way into the world, like some Biblical plague of locusts. And like locusts, the trylogogs start to scour the conservatory of all organic matter, intending to ultimately make it part of Ezel-zen-rezl. That includes all the exotic plants growing in the conservatory, every single one of the cultists trapped within, Professor Nidus, Dr Blaine…

And you.

The End.

"What is going on?" you hiss in anger and frustration. "Tell me everything!"

Dr Blaine gives you a condescending look and lets out a heavy sigh. "Very well. The Cult of Assimilation and the Cult of the Empty Sky. Each seeks to see their god ascend, and each has opened a portal to the dwelling place of their damned deity. But we must ensure that neither the hive mind that is Ezel-zen-rezl, the Lord of Swarms, nor the abomination Silenus, known as 'The Empty Sky,' rise to power this night."

Take **+1 INTELLECT.**

Knowing what you do now, how do you want to proceed?

> If you want to press home your attack against the followers of the Swarm God, turn to **281.**
>
> If you want to bring the battle to the worshippers of the Silenus, The Empty Sky, turn to **201.**
>
> If you want to ask Dr Blaine what the best course of action would be, turn to **189.**

Despite what she is telling you, and the look in her eyes, you find the strength to maintain eye contact with the seeress.

"Beware the shadow summoner," she says, her voice a rasping, guttural articulation that does not sound altogether human. "Seek the blade, though you will have to move heaven and earth to find it."

The old woman's shoulders suddenly sag, and she releases her grip on you, her hands falling into her lap. Her reading has clearly left her drained and she does not speak another word. Take the SECRET: *Wisdom of the Ancients*.

You, however, are left feeling very uneasy, believing that there are powers out there that have set their sights on you. Take +1 CLUE and the Weakness {HAUNTED}.

Turn to **219**.

As you are scouring the workstation, looking for anything that might tell you what Dr Waugh was doing here or why Dr Blaine had his suspicions about the astrophysicist, you come across a book that is open at a page covered with charts relating to the orbit of the moon. When you compare this to the list of dates, you realize that whoever has been working here – could it be Dr Waugh, as you suspect? – has calculated that an eclipse of the moon will occur later this very night. Take + 1 **CLUE**.

However, it is not only something on the lectern that attracts your attention – you also notice something lying on the floor under it. It is a [**KEY**]. There is nothing special about it, it is just a nondescript pin tumbler key, stamped with the number "120," but someone dropped it, and it must open something. The question is, what? But more importantly, where? You look around you at the space you're in and ponder how to solve the solution.

Turn to **170**.

Light suddenly blazes within the conservatory, throwing the shadows of the battling maniacs into stark relief against the walls. Cultists on both sides fall back in shock and awe as Dr Blaine ascends.

Arms outstretched on either side of his body, the old man's eyes begin to glow an intense white, and he slowly rises into the air, his feet dangling beneath him. Behind him, the shadows writhe across the wall and seem to coalesce into a writhing tentacle-like mass giving the impression that his body is cloaked in a robe of darkness.

"Nyarlathotep shall rise!" he cries, his voice booming

within the confines of the shattered conservatory, and a wave of nausea passes through you. "You shall all bow before the majesty of the Crawling Chaos!"

You had thought that the god you were here to stop rising to power this night was Ezel-zen-rezl, the Lord of Swarms. Then, it appeared that Silenus, the Empty Sky, might be the greater threat. Yet now it has been revealed that Nyarlathotep, the god of a thousand forms, posed the greatest danger all along.

But what are you going to do about it?

If you want to launch a surprise attack against Dr Blaine, turn to **289**.
If you would rather stand back and see what happens, turn to **224**.

182

"So, do you have it?" the academic asks, as eager as an excitable schoolboy.

"What?" you ask, still struggling to come to terms with the revelation that the man is not dead, as you had believed.

"The *blade*," he presses. Do you have it?"

If you have a [CEREMONIAL DAGGER], turn to **142**.
If not, turn to **162**.

Taking out the [BLACK TALON], you brandish it before you. Your incorporeal attackers appear to hesitate for a heartbeat, then swoop toward you. You can see them more clearly now, their insubstantial bodies giving the impression of gaping beaks and mist-trailing tails one moment, and outstretched wings and smoky talons the next. Their intention is clear. It is as if they consider you a trespasser here, and they cannot let such hubris go unpunished. You have no choice but to prepare for battle. But how can you battle something that appears to be little more than sentient smoke?

You may spend 1 RESOURCES at the start of each round to add 2 to your total for that round.

Round one: roll two dice and add your COMBAT and your WILLPOWER. If you have the {SECRET RITES} Ability, add 1. If the total is 14 or more, you win the first round.

Round two: roll two dice and add your COMBAT and your WILLPOWER. If you have the {SECRET RITES} Ability, add 1. If you won the first round, add 2. If your total is 15 or more, you win the second round.

> If you won the second round, turn to **113**.
> If you lost the second round, turn to **133**.

It is no good. While you are fighting to prevent the fulfilment of the prophecy, your enemy cares not for their own fate and are immune to psychology. No matter what grievous injuries you cause them, believing that ultimately there is nothing to live for other than a good death, they keep fighting when other more rational individuals would retreat to lick their wounds. It doesn't matter what gruesome deaths they witness their fellows suffer, nothing will deter them. The red mist has descended, and nothing can break its spell other than the total destruction of their enemy or their own downfall. And so, you soon find yourself fighting for your life against an enemy who literally has nothing to lose.

It doesn't matter what unearthly powers Dr Blaine brings to bear either. It soon becomes apparent that his academic rivals are both schooled in the sorcerous arts and wield reality-warping magics of their own. In the end, the two of you are overwhelmed by sheer force of numbers.

A god will rise to power in Arkham before the eclipse has passed, but you won't be there to discover which one.

The End.

Seeing the thing appear in the hole in the sky above Arkham has put an entirely different spin on things for you. Surely the emergence of such a monstrosity into the world is a far greater threat to Arkham, and defeating its devotees must become your new priority.

The thing is still probing at the edges of the tear in reality, and you realize then that you have been staring at the impossible abomination for some time. In fact, you now find yourself struggling to tear your gaze away from its monstrous magnificence.

Roll one die, and if you have either or both the {CURSED} or {HAUNTED} Weaknesses, deduct 1.

> If the total is equal to or less than your **SANITY**, turn to **258**.
> If the total is greater than your **SANITY**, turn to **196**.

Surveying the room, you consider the shapes under the sheets and try to work out which one is most likely to be the dead zoologist. Finding one that you think could be a match for Dr Blaine in terms of height and build, your pulse thudding in your ears, you stretch out a wary hand and pull back the sheet.

The body is that of a man, but one who is far too young and clean shaven. You do not know the cause of death, but he appears peaceful enough in his deathly repose. But then you see the raw wound on his shoulder and take a step back in horror.

Human teeth marks! A neat semi-circle of incisions in the young man's shoulder. Not only that but there is no blood or bruising to the surrounding flesh, meaning the bite was inflicted postmortem! Take -1 **SANITY** and the Secret: *Fancy a Bite?*

Throwing the sheet back over the mutilated body, you consider what your next action will be very carefully.

If you want to look for Dr Blaine in one of the refrigerated compartments, turn to **226**.
If you want to leave the morgue immediately, turn to **246**.

It soon becomes apparent that the book is number seven in a series about astronomy. The other nine volumes that complete the set stand at head height on a nearby shelf with a space for the book you now hold in your hands. You ponder what the whole series appears like together on the shelf, and what secrets they might contain.

The page the book had been left open at describes how to calculate the date of eclipses. However, there is nothing else on the reading table to suggest that the person reading the book actually did find out when the next eclipse would occur. Perhaps they took that piece of information with them when they left. Take **+1 CLUE.**

If you now want to read the green book, turn to **164**.

To take a closer look at the handwritten notebook, turn to **207**.

To leave the library and try the other door leading off from the corridor, turn to **25**.

To leave the library and return to central hallway of the house, turn to **247**.

You rap on the door and the voice within responds: "Enter."

You do so and find yourself in a study that is filled with bookcases and freestanding shelves. However, the shelves do not only bear books and string-tied bundles of academic papers, but also myriad glass jars. They are all filled with a yellowy green liquid within which can be seen all manner of curious specimens. The one thing they have in common is that they are all invertebrates – specifically of the taxonomic classification *insecta* – predominantly large beetles and overgrown, spine-encrusted stick insects.

A large man is standing in front of a workbench, with his back to you. As you enter, he draws a cloth over something that he is preoccupied with on a workbench and turns, looking you up and down. "May I help you?"

"I was looking for Professor Nidus," you tell him.

"Then you have come to the wrong place," he replies, peering at you through a pair of half-moon spectacles. "As the sign on the door says, I am Dr Milan Christopher."

Dr Christopher is not old, but he could be described as portly. He has a thick head of hair and a bushy beard, without a streak of gray in it. He is wearing blue overalls over his day-to-day clothes, and a red bowtie can be seen under his chin.

How will you respond?

Apologize and leave: turn to **208**.
Ask Dr Christopher about Professor Nidus: turn to **228**.
Ask him if he knows Dr Blaine: turn to **47**.
Ask what he's doing: turn to **67**.

"It matters not either way," Dr Blaine says, his words taking you somewhat by surprise. "For there is only one god who will rise this night in Arkham and that is the one whom I serve, the Haunter of the Dark, the Crawling Chaos, the Mighty Messenger – Nyarlathotep!"

Hearing the name spoken aloud, you feel your stomach knot and your gorge rise in response. It is all you can do to stop yourself being sick. If just hearing the name of Dr Blaine's deity can have such an instantaneous effect on a person, imagine what terrors the god could perpetrate if it were to be birthed upon the world.

At that moment, your mind is opened to the possibility of a world under the dominion of the Crawling Chaos, and it is enough to drive a sane individual mad.

Make a reason test. Roll one die and add your **INTELLECT**. If you have the {**STUDIOUS**} Ability, add 2. What's the result?

> Total of 8 or more: turn to **213**.
> 7 or less: turn to **252**.

"I'm looking for information about Abaddan House," you tell the librarian. "Do you know the place?"

ABADDAN
HOUSE

"I've not heard the name before," Carol says, "but give me a minute and I'll see if I can find anything."

She disappears into an office where the library's indexing system is to be found. It takes her more than a minute, but in the end, she emerges again and, stepping out from behind the counter, says, "If you'd like to follow me, I have found something that may be of interest."

Carol leads you to another floor and an area filled with map chests. Sliding open a drawer, she takes out a [BLUEPRINT].

"This is Abaddan House," she says, in hushed tones, laying the large piece of flimsy paper on a large, square table. "It's an old house located in the French Hill neighborhood. Its blueprint is stored here because it is a building of historical interest, since a previous owner turned the central courtyard into a huge, glass-domed conservatory."

Take + 1 CLUE and the SECRET: *The Librarian*.

You thank Carol for her help and start to peruse the plan, while she returns to her duty station. You do not believe it is coincidence that has led you to this place at this time, and you suspect that Abaddan House is somewhere you might want to investigate sooner rather than later.

If you want to take the [BLUEPRINT] with you, you will have to fold it up quickly and tuck it into your coat while nobody's looking, making a note of its catalog number, which is *108*.

You could lose yourself in the library for weeks, but you have a sneaking suspicion that time is of the essence if you are to get to the bottom of the mystery surrounding the fate of Dr Blaine. It's time to continue your search for clues elsewhere.

> Spend either **1 CLUE** or **1 RESOURCES**, or take + **1 DOOM**. Then turn to **140**.

The curious symbols put you in mind of Mesoamerican pictograms, but at the same time they look strange and quite different. But more than anything else, the shapes formed by the sigils remind you of the writhing limbs and bodies of deep-dwelling sea creatures.

"Very good," says Miriam Beecher, her eyebrows raised in what you take to be pleasant surprise. "It is an ancient language. Entire epochs have come and gone since it was first spoken, and its name is unpronounceable to the uninitiated. However, the keeper of this notebook has not actually written their notes in the language, they have merely used them as the basis of a code. The text as it stands is unintelligible."

For a moment there, you thought the secrets of [DR BLAINE'S NOTEBOOK] were about to be revealed to you, until Miriam informed you that the jotter is filled with nothing but incomprehensible gibberish. Perhaps Dr Blaine was mad.

But as you stare at the rows of symbols, you remember the note scribbled on the flyleaf. Turning back to it now, you see more of the same symbols, written faintly in pencil under Dr Blaine's name and place of work. Could this be the key to unlocking the code?

Property of Dr Blaine, Zoology Department, School of Life Sciences, Miskatonic University.

ꝗꝺꝺꝺꝺꝺꝺ ꝺ ꝺ

Turning back to the page Miriam Beecher was showing you, you flick between the two as you try to discern meaning from the seemingly meaningless.

[decorative coded script]

Can you decode [DR BLAINE'S NOTEBOOK]? If so, perhaps you can work out where you should go now.

> If you want to spend 1 CLUE to help you, turn to 285.
> If not, turn to 271.

192

Thumbing through the papers in a storage chest, Mr Peabody finally finds what he's looking for. "I don't have a copy of the plans of the house, but we do have this curio. It's a landscape gardener's plan of changes made to the estate by another member of the Nidus family back in the eighteenth century. It shows the proposed scheme to construct an underground

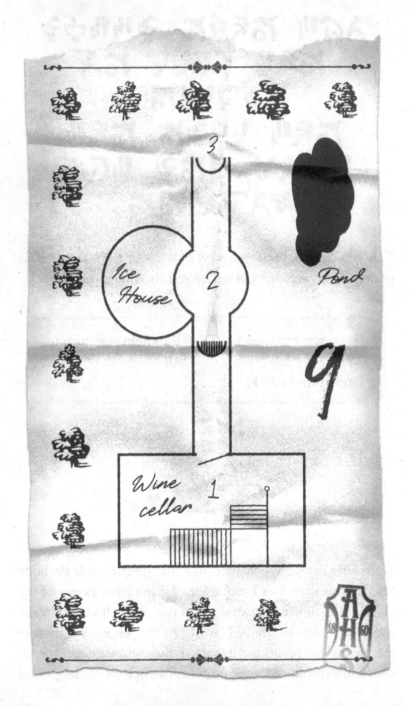

entrance to the house that connected the kitchens to an icehouse hidden under the lawns."

"May I borrow this?" you ask.

"Oh no, I can't let you take it away from here," Mr Peabody chides, "but you can make a copy if you like."

If you want to make a copy of the [GARDEN PLAN], add it to your inventory, along with the number that the original designer scrawled on the design, which is 9.

When you are done here, it's time to look elsewhere.

Take +2 DOOM and the SECRET: *The Historian*. You may spend 1 CLUE or 1 RESOURCES to reduce the DOOM penalty by 1; spend 2 CLUES or 2 RESOURCES to avoid adding any DOOM.

Turn to 140.

193

You bat at the bulbous insect bodies with your hands, unable to suppress your mewling cries of revulsion, but it is like trying to fight the wind. No matter what you do, you cannot escape the droning horde. Steadily backing toward the only exit from the morgue, in the end you give up trying the fight the swarm and instead turn tail and flee, bursting through the door. But as you are running back down the corridor from the nurse's station, before you can escape the hospital, several of the overgrown insects make good use of their monstrous mandibles and glistening stings. Lose -1 HEALTH.

It feels like there are powers at work behind the scenes, moving their pawns into position, as if they are preparing for war, or the fulfilment of some prophecy. And [DR BLAINE'S NOTEBOOK] is what got you caught up in this mystery in the first place. Perhaps there is something in there that could help you now. Or perhaps there is some message you have received that could grant you much needed insight.

If there is, you will have four numbers associated with this piece of information. Add them together and turn to the section that has the same number as the total.

> If you don't know of anything that could help you, turn to **259**.

You are in the central hallway of the house. Where do you want to look next?

> To explore the east wing of the house, turn to **234**.
> If you want to try the grand double doors to your left, turn to **267**.

The pinboard is covered with all manner of pictures, photographs, maps, and newspaper clippings. The pictures that grab your attention first: they are drawings of all manner of odd-looking creatures that look like they would be the subject of folklore studies rather than zoology. However, there are numerous artists' impressions of what appears to be a curious egg, and if the figures drawn beside them are anything to go by, it is gigantic, many times the height of a man. Take the SECRET: *A Curate's Egg*.

The photographs all seem to have been taken in a jungle, and feature a party of explorers. Among them is a much younger version of the man whose body is currently keeping you company in Dr Blaine's office. The collated newspaper articles all appear to relate to reports of unsubstantiated witness accounts of curious phenomena in and around Arkham.

Most prominent among the maps is one of Arkham itself. Various places have been circled using a red wax crayon, but most of them show no indication of what might be there. There are two circled locations, however, that pinpoint specific buildings. One is a house in French Hill district, and the other is Miskatonic University itself, where you are right now.

> Take +1 CLUE and turn to 215.

It is no good, you cannot tear your eyes from Silenus. The madness-inducing manifestation of the futility of all things is beginning to push its way through the rent in the cosmic veil. Humankind and its place in the world mean nothing, not when the very existence of the human race depends on the whim of insane gods that dwell beyond time and space, and who are not bound by the laws of physics that even stars and planets are beholden to.

A god will rise this night and that crazed deity shall be Silenus, the Empty Sky, the End of All Things. And you will continue to stare slack-jawed at your lord and master until Dr Blaine or one of the cultists puts you out of your misery. Failing that, you will remain standing there, your aching eyes never blinking once, until you collapse from thirst, malnutrition or exhaustion. And even then, you will continue to venerate your god as the life ebbs from you and you take your last breath.

Take the SECRET: *The Empty Sky.*

The End.

Heading left along the street you hurry after the old man, waving the notebook in the air as you call out to him. However, he appears deep in thought and is walking quickly, for he disappears around the corner of a grocery store at the end of the street without hearing you. You keep on to the end of the street, where it joins a busier thoroughfare. Cars, trucks and buses pass you in a constant stream of traffic, but there is no sign of the old man.

Could he have disappeared into one of the many buildings that line the street? Or perhaps he boarded a bus. No matter what the truth may be, you are unlikely to relocate him wandering up and down Peabody Avenue. You have a much better idea anyway.

You glance at the inscription inside the front cover once more and determine to make your way to Miskatonic University where either you can leave the notebook there for its owner to collect, or perhaps even bump into the mysterious Dr Blaine yourself.

Turn to **227**.

"They said you were dead," you protest.

"Who did?" asks Dr Blaine.

"The police. Detective Harden."

"Well, what do the police know?" the academic replies. "Very little, I can assure you."

Listening to Dr Blaine, you start to wonder how much of what you know is truth, and how much is lies, designed to obfuscate and confuse. Nothing more than smoke and mirrors.

Take -1 **INTELLECT** and the SECRET: *The First Casualty.*

> If you have [**WET SHOES**], turn to **209**.
> It not, turn to **182**.

It is no good. The old woman's stare is too intense, and what she is sharing with you too terrifying to bear. You pull your hands free of her grip at last. As you do so her shoulders sag and her hands drop into her lap. She looks utterly exhausted. She does not utter another word, but she does not need to. The truths she has revealed to you – and you know that they *are* truths – are enough to shake you to your core.

Lose -1 **SANITY**.

> Turn to **219**.

200

Your travails this night have taxed you more than you had realized. Despite adrenaline giving your beleaguered body a boost, it is not enough to enable you to carry yourself to safety. Exhausted, your body overwhelmed by what you have had to endure as much as your mind, you collapse before you can even make it out of the conservatory. But you do not witness the end when it comes, for by then you have been trampled underfoot by the battling cultists. But, while you might not have made it out, your actions have set in motion events that will ensure the people of Arkham, Massachusetts, live to fight another day.

Take the SECRET: *War of the Outer Gods.*

Final score: 2 stars.

The End.

201

You make the most of the momentary advantage you have been given and join with the devotees of the Swarm God in attacking the nihilistic interlopers.

However, having dispatched two of the invaders before they realize you are not with the Cult of the Swarm God, you suddenly find yourself face to face with another of the nihilists, who forces eye contact with you. You find yourself staring through the windows of the soul that belongs to an individual who is already lost to madness. And in her stare you see a reflection of the yawning portal and the Empty Sky that waits to welcome you on the other side.

Make a resolve test. Roll one die, add your **WILLPOWER** and your **SANITY**. You may spend **1 RESOURCES** to roll two dice and pick the highest. If you have the **{SECRET RITES}** Ability, add 1. What's the result?

> Total of 8 or more: turn to **253**.
> 7 or less: turn to **278**.

Keeping to the shadows of large yew hedges and away from any faculty building, you make your way through the grounds of the university, putting as much distance between yourself and the scene of the crime as possible. You are almost certain that Dr Blaine is dead but fear that the creature who might have killed him, and certainly tried to kill you, is still alive. Whatever is going on here, you have to get to the bottom of it, if only to prevent yourself becoming a victim of the gaunt, bat-winged night-hunter.

Not knowing what else to do, or where else to go, you set off for Ye Olde Magick Shoppe in Uptown.

> Turn to **171**.

You take out the [BRASS TELESCOPE] but what do you intend to do with it? Do you want to hit the ethereal creatures with it? Are you going to look at them through it, and make them appear even bigger? You stand there, frozen by indecision, as the wraithlike creatures swoop toward you. Their intention is clear. It is as if they consider you a trespasser here, and they cannot let such hubris go unpunished. You have no choice but to prepare for battle. But how can you battle something that appears to be little more than sentient smoke?

You may spend 1 RESOURCES at the start of each round to add 2 to your total for that round.

Round one: roll two dice and add your COMBAT and your WILLPOWER. If you have the {SECRET RITES} Ability, add 1. If the total is 16 or more, you win the first round.

Round two: roll two dice and add your COMBAT and your WILLPOWER. If you have the {SECRET RITES} Ability, add 1. If you won the first round, add 2. If your total is 17 or more, you win the second round.

> If you won the second round, turn to 113.
> If you lost the second round, turn to 133.

You explain to the duty officer that you want to help find Dr Blaine's killer.

"Who told you he was dead?" asks the cop, giving you a suspicious look.

You tell him that news of the academic's sudden death has spread like wildfire round Miskatonic University, but internally you are already starting to doubt your decision to come to the Police Station.

"If I were you, I'd get lost," the duty officer suggests. "And if I see you round here again, I might be tempted to put you in the cells for the night the wasting police time."

You decide that there is nothing to be gained by pursuing your inquiries here, and so try to think of somewhere else you could look.

> Spend either **1 CLUE** or **1 RESOURCES** or take **+ 1 DOOM**. Then turn to **140**.

Your pulse thudding in your ears, you prepare to battle the beetle-like wasps.

You may spend **1 RESOURCES** at the start of each round to add 2 to your total for that round.

Round one: roll two dice and add your **COMBAT**. If you have the Weakness {**FEAR OF INSECTS**} deduct 2. If the total is 13 or more, you win the first round. If you lose the first round, Lose - **1 HEALTH**.

Round two: roll two dice and add your **COMBAT**. If you have the Weakness {**FEAR OF INSECTS**} deduct 2. If you won the first round, add 2. If your total is 14 or more, you win the second round.

> If you won the second round, turn to **245**.
> If you lost the second round, turn to **225**.

206

Waves of insanity-inducing power pulse from the shadow-bound sorcerer, slowly peeling away the layers of your mind as if it were an onion, until the very core of your being is exposed to the truth of what you naively call "reality." Humankind and its place in the world mean nothing, not when the very existence of the human race depends on the whim of insane gods that dwell beyond time and space, and who are not bound by the laws of physics that even stars and planets are beholden to.

A god will rise this night and that madness-inducing deity shall be Nyarlathotep, the Crawling Chaos, thanks to the machinations of his soul-bound servant, Dr Blaine, and his puppet pawn. You! You will sing the praises of the god of a thousand faces until your throat is raw from your declamations and your body fails, having neglected to eat or drink, so in awe are you of your new master.

Take the SECRET: *The Crawling Chaos.*
The End.

Pouring over the handwritten notes, you learn that they were made by one Archibald Nidus and chronicle his travels in Central America. It seems he spent years exploring an ancient cave system, never-before-delved by humans, that lies beneath those jungle-smothered lands home, hunting for one artifact in particular.

But more intriguing than that is the legend Archibald recorded in the notebook concerning three rival gods battling for domination of the world. One of these is named Silenus, or "The Empty Sky", a being that dwells beyond the known universe, in a place that has been dead for eons. It is described as looking like a mass of gray smoke that stretches throughout space, but through which claws, wings, jaws, and countless eyes, can be seen. It is also possessed of long tendrils that suck the life from anything organic they encounter.

You can't help thinking that this book could be one of the most valuable in the whole library and, since it is small, you pop [ARCHIBALD'S ACCOUNT] into your pocket.

Take +1 CLUE and +1 RESOURCES.

> Turn to **9**.

Leaving the entomologist's room, where do you want to go now?

> If you want to look for Professor Nidus, turn to **298**.
> If you would prefer to leave the Science Building, turn to **140**.

"But your body was taken to St Mary's Hospital. I followed it there," you protest. "I went to the morgue myself."

As you start to recount what happened at the hospital, you recall the feeling of unease you had upon entering the mortuary and feel the gooseflesh rise on your arms as you do so. Remembering what happened there, down among the dead men, you feel your mind reel. Lose - **1 SANITY**.

"What was taken to the morgue was a mere simulacrum. And it served its purpose admirably."

A simulacrum? What is the man talking about? Is he mad? Or is it you who's mad?

The longer this goes on, the more you can feel your sanity slowly slipping away. Spend **1 RESOURCES** or lose another - **1 SANITY**.

> Turn to **182**.

The Historical Society is to be found in the Southside neighborhood of Arkham, headquartered in a building that originally belonged to Uriah Crawford, a minister who lived in the town during the witchcraft trials of the late seventeenth century. Take the SECRET: *Location Eight.*

Its current curator, Mr Peabody, welcomes you with a smile and invites you in. As you do as you are bidden and enter the wonderful archive that is the Historical Society, he asks what brings you here at this time of night.

Keeping your answer vague you say, "I am researching old families of Arkham, and I wondered if you had any information that might help me."

"Which old families in particular?" Mr Peabody asks, his expression suddenly inscrutable.

"The Waugh family. Blaine. Maybe Nidus?"

"Ah, now the Nidus family I have heard of," he says excitedly. "They have a place in French Hill. Abaddan House, that's it. The family have lived here for centuries, and I believe the current owner of the house works at the University. Her father was a renowned explorer and azrchaeologist, but rumor has it that he discovered something in the jungles of Central America."

"What did he find?" you ask.

"That I don't know, but I do know that he also carried out major renovation works to the house, converting part of it into a grand conservatory. I think there might be a plan of the grounds somewhere. I'm sure it wouldn't take me long to find it, if you would like to see it."

If you want to wait while Mr Peabody looks for the plan, turn to **192**.

If you think your time would be better spent visiting somewhere else in the hunt for clues, take **+1 DOOM** and turn to **140**. You may spend either **1 CLUE** or **1 RESOURCES** to avoid this **DOOM** penalty.

Even though you do not have all the letters, you are able to work out those that are missing and make sense of what Dr Blaine has written here. That is, you can make sense of the words. if not the meaning.

> *When the moon in darkness dies,*
> *Then a new god shall arise.*
> *One from three shall claim the prize.*
> *One called from the burning pit,*
> *One that seeks the veil to split,*
> *The last the child, its egg forfeit.*

They do say a little knowledge is a dangerous thing, while ignorance is bliss. Never has that felt truer than it does now.

Take **+1 CLUE** but **-1 SANITY**, and the SECRET: *Hidden Three*.

Turning to another page, you start to decode what is

written there, now that you have a better understanding of the cypher. This time you find yourself reading Dr Blaine's private thoughts about two of his colleagues, a Professor Nidus from the Life Sciences Department, and one Dr Waugh, an astrophysicist who works at the Warren Observatory.

Turn to **141**.

Taking out the [BRASS TELESCOPE], you are rather taken aback when the cultists stumble to a halt, giving each other uncomfortable glances and muttering among themselves. What could be the significance of the object? And why has its appearance unsettled the Disciples of the Swarm?

Turn to **13**.

A little knowledge can most definitely be a dangerous thing, but it may also be your way out of this mess. For knowing the name of something is the first step toward defeating it. And such understanding makes the madness that is overtaking Abaddan House seem that much less of a threat to you personally.

> **Gain + 1 SANITY** and turn to **181**.

You run to the door and go to push it open, only to be met by resistance. You push harder, but the door will not budge. Desperate now, taking hold of the handle, you rattle the door hard, but get nowhere. It would appear you are trapped!

The buzzing intensifies and you turn to find yourself surrounded by the swarm. You get the impression of hornet-like bodies, bulging multi-faceted eyes, bristly black carapaces, whirring wings, champing mouthparts, and glistening spear-tip stingers. The relentless droning of the creatures fills your skull. You feel the creatures crawling about all over you – in your hair, around your mouth, over your eyes – and some of them sting you, causing you to cry out in agony. Where their stings penetrate your flesh, it feels like your skin has been set on fire! Lose - **1 HEALTH** and -**1 COMBAT**.

You have no choice but to fight back as best you can. You may spend **1 RESOURCES** at the start of each round to add 2 to your total for that round.

Round one: roll two dice and add your **COMBAT** and your **INTELLECT**. If the total is 10 or more, you win the first round.

Round two: roll two dice and add your **COMBAT** and your **INTELLECT**. If you won the first round, add 2. If your total is 11 or more, you win the second round.

> If you won the second round, turn to **290**.
> If you lost the second round, turn to **274**.

215

You are abruptly aware of pounding footsteps coming down the corridor toward the study and in the next instant four police officers burst into the room, followed by a jittery-looking member of the Science Building's secretarial staff.

"Hands in the air!" the burly sergeant leading the cops shout, and you do as he says. His eyes flick between you and the body in the chair, and appalled horror creeps across his face with what feels like agonizing slowness.

> Turn to **262**.

216

Taking out the blueprint and the landscape gardener's plan, you consider the two together by the light of the myriad stars of the Milky Way twinkling across the firmament above you. You should have one number associated with each item. If so, divide the larger number by the smaller number and turn to the section that is the same as the answer.

If you do not know where to turn next, turn to **15**.

217

You feel Dr Blaine's command as a physical force that tugs at both your body and mind. Shutting your eyes tight and gritting your teeth leaves you with an uncomfortable sensation that feels like the ebbing of a headache.

"Do not try your tricks on me!" you snarl at the sorcerer.

You fix him with a piercing look, as if to say, don't think I won't turn on you in an instant if I believe I must, in order to protect myself.

Dr Blaine returns your gaze, and you imagine his reply: "We are allies of convenience only. Do not dare cross me."

But there is still the matter of your would-be attacker to deal with.

Turn to **201**.

Your heartrate rising, you nevertheless manage to keep your growing feelings of alarm in check as you consider what might be the best approach, if you want to defeat the ascendant sorcerer, as Dr Blaine turns back to wiping out the battling cultists.

> If you want to attack him while his attention is focused elsewhere, turn to **289**.
> If you think you might have some arcane artifact that you could use against him, turn to **296**.

You have been in the holding cell for an hour when a police officer appears before the bars and calls your name.

"Looks like you have a guardian angel," he says, unlocking the cell door. Seeing the quizzical look on your face he adds, "Someone has bailed you out."

"Who?" you ask.

"I'm not at liberty to say, but if I were you, I wouldn't waste time worrying about who got me out of jail. I'd skedaddle as fast as I could."

That sounds like good advice and before you know it you are wandering the streets of Easttown as the streetlamps come on, wondering what to do now.

It feels like there are powers at work behind the

scenes, moving their pawns into position, as if they are preparing for war, or the fulfilment of some prophecy. And [DR BLAINE'S NOTEBOOK] is what got you caught up in this mystery in the first place. Perhaps there is something in there that could help you now. Or perhaps there is some message you have received that could grant you much needed insight.

If there is, you will have four numbers associated with this piece of information. Add them together and turn to the section that has the same number as the total.

If you don't know anything that could help you, turn to **259**.

220

You suddenly find yourself surrounded by a horde of hideous insects. You try not to look at them too closely, but you get the impression of hornet-like bodies, bulging multi-faceted eyes, bristly black carapaces, whirring wings, snapping mandibles and iridescent, spear-tip stingers. The relentless droning fills your head. You feel the creatures crawling about all over you – in your hair, around your mouth, over your eyes – and stifle a cry of revulsion. Were you to open your mouth, some of the horrid things might actually get inside.

How can you fight a swarm of insects? You're about to find out. You may spend **1 RESOURCES** at the start of each round to add 2 to your total for that round.

Round one: roll two dice and add your **COMBAT** and your **INTELLECT**. If the total is 10 or more, you win the first round.

Round two: roll two dice and add your **COMBAT** and your **INTELLECT**. If you won the first round, add 2. If your total is 11 or more, you win the second round.

> If you won the second round, turn to **233**.
> If you lost the second round, turn to **193**.

221

Without giving them any warning, you throw yourself at the nearest cultists, laying about you and knocking several to the floor before they even know what is going on. Take **+1 COMBAT**.

However, it doesn't take their fellows long to muster an effective defense and they come for your then. Seeing how you have blown his cover, Dr Blaine has little choice but to join you in battling the devotees of the Swarm God and so the two of you engage in battle, using every weapon you have at your disposal.

This is going to be a tough fight! You may spend **1 RESOURCES** at the start of each round to add 2 to your total for that round.

Round one: roll two dice and add your **COMBAT**. If you have the {**AGILE**} Ability, add 1. If the total is 15 or more, you win the first round.

Round two: roll two dice and add your **COMBAT**. If you have the {AGILE} Ability, add 1. If you won the first round, add 2. If your total is 16 or more, you win the second round.

> If you won the second round, turn to **269**.
> If you lost the second round, turn to **257**.

222

Showing the cop on duty [DETECTIVE HARDEN'S CARD], you ask to see Detective Harden. A few minutes later the detective appears and ushers you into an interview room.

"What have you got for me?" he asks.

> If you want to spend **1 CLUE** to share what you have discovered so far with Detective Harden, turn to **261**.
> If not, turn to **241**.

223

You open fire at the creatures, but the bullets just seen to pass straight through the creatures, leaving nothing more than whirling eddies in the smoky substance of their impossible bodies.

You begin to fear that you have met your match in these ethereal entities. Lose - **1 WILLPOWER.**

> Turn to **64.**

224

In the face of such madness, you crave understanding. Staring at the ascendant sorcerer, you articulate your desperate need for the truth. "What are you doing?"

Dr Blaine turns his burning gaze upon you and regards you with pupilless eyes, as if he is regarding a pet. "Ah, my useful idiot," he says, the too-wide smile spreading across this bearded face revealing too many teeth. "You seek understanding. Very well, knowledge shall be my final gift to you."

Having been cowed by Dr Blaine's sudden ascension, the cultists of the Swarm God and the Empty Sky are beginning to recover themselves.

"It began with Professor Nidus and her plan to use the vessel her father discovered in the jungles of Central America to summon Ezel-zen-rezl into the world. My master could not allow another god to rise to power in Arkham, and so I sought to subvert her summoning ritual so that it would strengthen Nyarlathotep's influence over the town instead. However, due to the magical wards she had put in place around Abaddan House" – he indicates your surroundings with a sweep of his burning gaze – "I was prevented from entering the place where the ritual would be enacted. That is where you came in. I left a trail of breadcrumbs for you to follow, so that you would provide me with the means to breach those wards and thereby accomplish my great work."

"But what of the Cult of the Empty Sky?" you ask.

"I can only imagine that your theft of the blade encouraged them to bring forward their own plans, probably with the intention of corrupting Nidus's ritual themselves, so that they might fulfil the prophecy in favor of their own dark master."

The blade! It all comes back to the Blade of Ark'at! If it is such a potent artifact, could you use it to stop any of the warring deities from gaining the upper hand?

Confusion reigns within the conservatory, with some of the rival cultists appearing to form temporary alliances, suddenly finding they have a common enemy in Nyarlathotep's herald, while others still seem determined to not stop until the other side has been eradicated utterly. All the while, insects throng the space in buzzing clouds, while far above Arkham, monstrous appendages probe the periphery of the portal that has formed at the heart of the eclipse.

What do you want to do?

Flee from this place as fast as you can: turn to **260**.
Attack Dr Blaine yourself: turn to **77**.
Focus your attention on trying to stop the summoning of Ezel-zen-rezl: turn to **157**.
Concentrate on stopping the emergence of Silenus, the Empty Sky: turn to **185**.
Work to engineer the mutual destruction of both sides: turn to **51**.
Make the ultimate sacrifice in order to deny the schemes of the Outer Gods vying for power in this place: turn to **50**.

You do your best to fend off the giant insects, but no matter how hard you struggle they still manage to evade your guard and plunge their vicious stingers into your body again and again. Each time it happens it feels like you are being stabbed by someone wielding a railway spike that has been heated in a blacksmith's forge.

In the end, knowing that you cannot defeat them, you give up trying to harm them and stumble through the house, searching for a way out. But the insects' poison is already coursing through your body and every step you take simply sends it through your bloodstream with even greater rapidity. As the front door, and a means of escape, comes within sight, your vision blurs, your chest constricts and, gasping for breath, you collapse onto the hallway carpet. Your vision grays to black, and somewhere at the edge of hearing, as if coming from very far off, you can make out the insistent droning of insects...

The End.

Your breath mists in the cold air of the morgue. For some reason, the hatches are numbered from *#61* to *#90*, rather than starting at *#1*. Perhaps there is one that is of particular interest to you.

As you are carefully considering which door to open, you become aware of a faint hum. It could be the distant echo of some piece of hospital machinery, but the sound intrigues you and you try to discern precisely where it is coming from. It doesn't take you long to pinpoint the source of the sound. It is coming from behind door *#78*.

> If you want to risk opening the drawer, turn to **78**.
> If you want to leave the morgue without further delay, turn to **246**.

By the time you arrive at Miskatonic University, dusk is falling and the chill in the air leeches the warmth from your bones. You make your way along paved paths that crisscross carefully tended lawns between the gray stone academic buildings, following signs until you reach the part of the campus where the School of Life Sciences is located. From there, you make your way through dimly lit corridors, redolent with the smell of decaying wood pulp and tobacco smoke, until you find yourself in a corridor at the top of the building, standing before a walnut-paneled door. Secured to the door is a brass name plaque:

Dr D. Blaine
Department of Zoology

Lying on the carpeted floor of the corridor is a [HANDKERCHIEF]. Bending down, you pick it up and see that it bears the embroidered monogram *DB*. Add the [HANDKERCHIEF] to your Character Sheet, if you wish.

You knock on the door, which creaks open at your touch. Even though no one welcomes you, or beckons you to enter, you step into the zoologist's study, nonetheless. If Dr Blaine isn't there, you can leave the notebook for him here.

A large mahogany desk dominates the room, which is also crammed with bookcases and glass-fronted cabinets that make the space appear more cramped than it really is. Sat at a chair behind the desk, and facing the door, you recognize the gray-haired old man you saw arguing earlier with the spiky woman. Except that he isn't sitting, rather he is sprawled in his seat, with his head is thrown back so that he is staring at the ceiling.

"Dr Blaine?" you say, your voice sounding strangely loud as it cuts through the musty ticking-clock stillness of the room.

The banging of a window draws your attention from the motionless body to the open aperture opposite you, beyond the desk. Your mind racing, you start to come up with all sorts of questions and possible explanations regarding the scene in front of you. Is Dr Blaine dead? Did someone attack him and then make their escape through the window? You certainly didn't pass anyone on the way to his office, which lies at the end of a long corridor. And if someone did attack him, why? Were they looking for something and, if so, did they find it?

You only have a moment to decide what you want to do.

> To check if the old man is still alive, turn to **10**.
> To run to the open window, turn to **52**.
> To search the study for clues, turn to **33**.

228

"Do you know Professor Nidus?" you ask Dr Christopher.

"But of course," the entomologist replies. "She is an important figure within the Department."

"Do you know where I might find her then?"

The rotund man gives you an appraising look over the top of his half-moon glasses. "Might I ask why you are looking for her?"

"Yes, of course. I need her help with returning a notebook to its rightful owner."

Make a trustworthiness test. Roll one die and add your **WILLPOWER**. You may spend **1 RESOURCES** to roll two dice and pick the highest. If you have the **{PARANOID}** Weakness, deduct 1 from the total, and if you have the **{CRIMINAL}** Weakness, deduct 1 as well. What's the result?

> Total of 8 or more: turn to **248**.
> 7 or less: turn to **27**.

229

Focusing your mind, you prepare to fight fire with fire. But as you draw on your own sorcerous power, so Dr Blaine's preternatural senses alert him to what you are doing.

"Impudent worm," the inhuman sorcerer snarls, his pupilless gaze white-hot. "You dare to challenge me?"

With that he points at you and one of the writhing tentacle shadows reaches for you. At the same time, you feel something cold and muscular wrap about your body and start to squeeze. There is nothing you can do as the sorcerer's shadow-limb pulls tighter and tighter. Bones break and blood spurts from ruptures in your flesh until you mercifully black out.

The End.

230

Your mind awhirl, you do not know what else to say. But Dr Blaine fills the silence for you. "Who do you think it was that bailed you out of jail?"

Slowly things are starting to make sense, even if that semblance of sense seems closer to madness. If Dr Blaine has been observing you from a safe distance this night, who else would have known you had been taken to the Police Station in the first place other than him? But if he is still alive, who – or what – was it that everyone took to be the dead Dr Blaine?

Turn to **182**.

231

"I've never seen anything like them before," you tell Miriam. "I was hoping you might be able to tell me what they are."

"Take a look at them again," says the owner of Ye Old Magick Shoppe. "Do you see anything now?"

You stare at the curious sigils until they start to swirl on the page before you.

Make a pattern recognition test. Roll one die and add your **INTELLECT**. You can spend **1 CLUE** to roll two dice and pick the highest. And if you have the {ARCANE STUDIES} Ability, add 1 as well.

What is the result?

> 8 or higher: turn to **251**.
> 7 or less: turn to **271**.

There is suddenly a flare of light from beside you, and you instinctively shut your eyes against its brilliance. You hear cries of shock, dismay, and pain, and feel the cultists release their hold on you. Most noticeably of all, the chanting filling the conservatory falters for the first time since you entered this place.

The acrid stink of burning hair assails your nostrils and you open your eyes again. Your attackers lie in broken heaps on the floor of the conservatory, unmoving.

A scream suddenly rises from the woman standing atop the stone platform, that embodies all the rage and frustration of the high priestess. Following her gaze, beyond the glass panels that form the roof of the conservatory you can see the round white orb of the moon, set amid a myriad of diamond stars. But at the same time, you can see the shadow of the Earth is starting to creep across the face of the moon. What is the significance of this to cause such a reaction in Professor Nidus? Did her ritual need to be completed before the eclipse occurred?

In the next moment, you have your answer. There is something approaching Abaddan House from out of the night's sky, and as it draws closer, so the light that fills the conservatory bathes the hideous, impossible monstrosity in a jaundice-yellow glow. You have seen too many unbelievable things this night, but nothing like what is approaching the Cult of Assimilation's stronghold now. In the most basic sense, it looks like a bird, in that it has great outstretched wings and a beak-like mouth. But in truth its wings are colossal, like those of some giant bat, and its mouth is a gaping maw lined with elongated fangs.

But there is something else even more unsettling about the creature than its appearance. It seems not to be quite there, for when you try to focus on it, its body appears blurred, as if it is out of focus or made from some incorporeal substance, such as mist or maybe smoke. As the creature approaches from out of the night, it gives a screeching cry that can be heard quite clearly inside the cult's meeting place. It sounds like it foretells the doom of all those corralled within.

With every beat of the avian's wings comes another shocking revelation. For riding on the back of the great beast is a man.

"Dr Waugh," hisses Dr Blaine at your side. "He's not been idle either."

But the worst is yet to come. As you and everyone else within the conservatory, it would seem, awaits the arrival of the errant astrophysicist, the Earth's obstruction of the sun's light becomes total, and the moon goes black.

With the next blink of your eyes, something changes. The hole in the sky where the moon hangs, appears to become exactly that. Where you know a dwarf planet hangs in orbit a quarter of a million miles above the Earth, all you can see now is a yawning void, and not the void of space but the void of a hole between realities. Where there should be the Earth's bound satellite there is now a gaping portal, an opening between one universe and another, alien cosmos. Within the gateway between realities, something moves. Something vast. An entity of claws, multiple distended jaws and myriad eyes, emerging from the interstellar mists of dead nebulae.

Make a resolve test. Roll one die, add your **WILLPOWER** and your **SANITY**. You may spend 1 **RESOURCES** to roll two dice and pick the highest. What's the result?

Total of 10 or more: turn to **292**.
9 or less: turn to **37**.

233

Grabbing what you find to hand – and sending a pile of scalpels and other sterilized tools clattering to the floor in the process – you proceed to swat at the bulbous insects with the enameled metal tray that you now have grasped in both hands. Buzzing things are sent tumbling to the floor, their wings broken, while others are splatted between the tray and the wall, or the tray and the trolleys. Eventually, those that remain leave you alone and alight on the shrouded corpses or bump against the shaded lamps that bathe the morgue in a jaundiced yellow light. Take + **1 COMBAT**.

Dr Blaine's body isn't going to reveal anything more now. Take + **1 CLUE**.

You cannot bear to remain in St Mary's Hospital a moment

longer and run from the place as fast as your feet will carry you.

It feels like there are powers at work behind the scenes, moving their pawns into position, as if they are preparing for war, or the fulfilment of some prophecy. And [DR BLAINE'S NOTEBOOK] is what got you caught up in this mystery in the first place. Perhaps there is something in there that could help you now. Or perhaps there is some message you have received that could grant you much needed insight.

If there is, you will have four numbers associated with this piece of information. Add them together and turn to the section that has the same number as the total.

> If you don't know of anything that could help you, turn to **259**.

You are in the east wing of the house. The decor has the air of the previous century about it. Two doors lead off from the corridor, one to the left and one further along to the right.

> If you want to try the door to the left, turn to **25**.
> If you want to try the door to the right, turn to **85**.
> If you want to return to the central hallway, turn to **247**.

In the face of the creature's aggressive assault and the sheer horror of its incomprehensible existence, you stumble and succumb to its shredding claws, suffering a savage wound. It may look like a hallucination from a nightmare, but the monster's claws are still perfectly capable of harming you. Lose - 1 HEALTH.

The creature looms before you, as if preparing its killing strike, and you stagger away. Caught between the inexorable advance of the horror and the precipitous drop to the graveled ground more than thirty feet below, you grab hold of a protruding ornamental roof spike.

Just when you think your time has come, you hear the screech of brakes from below, followed by shouts and the slamming of car doors. The monster turns its faceless head, pinpointing the source of the clamor and, with one final angry hiss, takes to the air, powerful beats of its enormous wings carrying it away into the deepening darkness of the night.

Badly shaken by your encounter with the beast, you consider your options. From your vantage point you can see that further along the roof ridge, iron-grilled steps lead to a fire escape at the back of the building that would take you back to ground level. Alternatively, you could return the way you came, through the window of Dr Blaine's study.

What's it to be?

If you want to climb down the fire escape, turn to **90**.
If you want to re-enter Dr Blaine's study via the window, turn to **255**.

Whether you can find another way into Abaddan House or not depends on how well you know the layout of the property and its grounds.

If you have both a [BLUEPRINT] and a [GARDEN PLAN], turn to **216**.
If not, you and Dr Blaine and going to have to resort to a less subtle method: turn to **15**.

You feel the power of Dr Blaine's words and find yourself compelled to obey. In that instant it is as if you are an impotent observer watching what unfolds from within the prison of your own body. You bring the blade down, striking the stunned nihilist in the chest, and watch, helpless, as the chitinous matter it is made from smashes through his ribcage.

The cultist drops to the ground, staring eyes locked on yours, and then is still. You feel Dr Blaine's hold on you relax and you almost drop to your knees, your body shaking in shock. Lose -**1** **SANITY** and gain the Weakness {CURSED}.

But you can't worry about the death of one insane cultist. This is what you are here to do – stop either faction from seeing the accursed prophecy being fulfilled in their favor.

What do you want to do?

Confront the Cult of Assimilation: turn to **281**.
Continue to battle the cultists of the Empty Sky: turn to **201**.
Stand back at see what happens: turn to **181**.

Fighting your way through the insects, you make it to the top of the stone dais where Professor Nidus greets you will a look of abject surprise and a scream of anger. But she gives away her greatest secret when she glances down at the vessel that stands on the plinth between the two of you.

As you watch, a large black insect, like some grotesque amalgam of a scarab beetle and a tarantula hawk, emerges from the mouth of the pot and buzzes its wings before taking off and joining the throng that fills the air around you. You can see the probing antennae of another bug at the lip of the pot, but before it can escape, you pick up the vessel with both hands and hurl it to the ground. It hits the edge of the stone dais and explodes into a cloud of red terracotta shards and brick dust.

Professor Nidus shrieks again, this time in horror, and

reaches for you with fingers that have transformed into hooked talons. But before she can throw herself upon you, the swarm descends. Clearly, you have disrupted the ritual and now the high priestess of the swarm suffers the consequences. But rather than try to sting her or bite her flesh with their scissoring mouthparts, the creatures land on her and crawl into any opening they can find, including her nostrils, her mouth, and even her ears. The wretched woman's screams become choking coughs. She stumbles backward from the dais, tumbling down the steps and landing awkwardly on the stone-flagged floor, where the grotesque insects continue to burrow into her body.

Having thwarted the Cult of Assimilation, by turning Professor Nidus's plans against her, what do you want to do now?

Save yourself and flee from this place as fast as you can: turn to **150**.

Attack Dr Blaine: turn to **77**.

Turn your attention to stopping the emergence of Silenus: turn to **249**.

238

As you climb to the top of Crane Hill, before you can even reach the Gerald Warren Astronomical Observatory, you are intercepted by a pair of incorporeal creatures that look like wisps of smoke that have been granted autonomous control of their insubstantial bodies. Take the SECRET: *Location Seven.*

Their intention is clear, and you have no choice but to defend yourself.

You may spend **1 RESOURCES** at the start of each round to add 2 to your total for that round.

Round one: roll two dice and add your **COMBAT** and your **WILLPOWER**. If you have the {**SECRET RITES**} Ability, add 1. If the total is 14 or more, you win the first round.

Round two: roll two dice and add your **COMBAT** and your **WILLPOWER**. If you have the {**SECRET RITES**} Ability, add 1. If you won the first round, add 2. If your total is 15 or more, you win the second round.

> If you won both rounds, turn to **17**.
> If you lost one or more rounds, turn to **46**.

Your mind racing, you try to come up with a way to defend yourself against the droning horde, as the cloud of buzzing bugs bears down on you.

Do you have anything you could use to improvise an effective weapon?

> If you have a [LIGHTER] and either a bottle of [WHISKEY] or [SWABBING ALCOHOL], turn to **174**.
>
> If you do not have enough, or any, of these items, turn to **254**.

"I want to do what I can to help find Dr Blaine's killer," you tell the detective.

"The best thing you can do is tell me anything you know," Harden replies. "I thought you might have come here because you had some information for me."

> If you want to spend **1 CLUE** to share what you have discovered, turn to **261**.
>
> If not, it's time to take your investigations elsewhere; take **+1 DOOM** and turn to **140**.

You emerge from the darkness and call out to the police officers.

> If you have the {POLICE} or {DETECTIVE} Ability, turn to **297**.

"Halt!" a burly sergeant shouts, catching sight of you. "Hands in the air!"

You do as he says and he looks you up and down, suspicion in his eyes. You dread to think how you appear after your run-in with the rooftop hunter. Two of the cops head into the building while the fourth, a young rookie by the look of things, remains with the sergeant.

"Who are you and what are you doing here?" the sergeant asks gruffly.

You tell him your name and make up a fictitious class in animal behavior studies that you've been attending. Then you ask him the same thing: what are the police doing here?

"We've had reports of a disturbance. We think one of the professors has been attacked. Have you seen anything?"

The sergeant doesn't once take his eyes off your face as you decide, in this case, that honesty is probably not the best policy and repeat that you have just been atteznding a lecture on the fishmen of the Devil's Reef. The real question is, does he believe you?

Make a duping test. Roll one die and add your **INTELLECT**. You can spend **1 RESOURCES** to roll two dice and pick the highest. What's the result?

Total of 8 or more: turn to **5**.
7 or less: turn to **262**.

Many of the buildings are mere off-cuts of wood, lacking any details whatsoever. However, others have been shaped to look like the places they represent and have been painted accordingly. It's obvious why some landmarks have been picked out by the model-maker, but you cannot discern the reasoning behind the inclusion of other peculiar places. There is the Miskatonic University, complete with a model of the Warren Observatory and the Orne Library. Then there is the Historical Society in Arkham's Southside neighborhood. A less obvious inclusion is Ye Olde Magick Shoppe, in Uptown, and another is a large house in French Hill.

Moving on from the model of the town, you start to examine the star charts pinned to the corkboards that cover one wall of Dr Waugh's office. One of them isn't a star chart at all, but a drawing of what would appear to be a constellation, although it is not one you are familiar with. That said, as you stare at it, it does begin to appear slightly familiar. But the only other thing you have looked at in any detail since entering Dr Waugh's private sanctum is the model of Arkham.

Taking the drawing of the constellation from the wall, you return to the model, holding one up before the other. Unbelievably, the stars of the constellation correspond to the locations highlighted on the miniature recreation of Arkham.

There is only one highlighted location that doesn't line up with the stars that make up the constellation and that is the French Hill house.

Returning to the wall of charts, you manage to line up the drawing with stars on a large map of the heavens. At the point that corresponds to where the French Hill house stands on the three-dimensional representation of the town, there is nothing on the star map at all – nothing but the empty blackness of space.

You do not know what it all means, but the knowledge that Dr Waugh has successfully mapped a constellation that was previously unknown to you onto the town of Arkham so accurately leaves you feeling deeply unsettled. And where does the French Hill house fit into it? And what are the implications if the equivalent area of space is devoid of anything whatsoever?

Thinking it might be helpful to you nonetheless, you find a piece of paper and a pencil on a desk and make your own map of the town plan and the locations marked upon it. Add the [TOWN MAP] to your Character Sheet and take +2 CLUES.

It is as you are making your sketch map that you catch sight of a wooden box that has been shoved under the desk. From the way it is half sticking out, it looks like whoever put it there did so quickly before someone else could see it, or as if they were forced to leave the office in a hurry.

> If you want to take a look inside the box, turn to **263**.
>
> If you want to leave well alone and get back to looking for Dr Waugh, turn to **14**.

244

"But I saw your body," you say, suddenly gabbling. "You were dead."

The enigmatic Dr Blaine arches one eyebrow. "Was I?"

"You *looked* like you were dead."

"It would seem that you cannot always trust your own eyesight," he says, smiling wryly.

> If you have [INKY FINGERS], turn to **230**.
> If you have [WET SHOES], turn to **209**.
> If you do not have either of these, turn to **182**.

245

You bat at the overgrown insects using anything and everything you can, but they are relentless. To avoid their lancing stings, you back away from them. As you do so, you pass a painting of a horse hung on the wall to your left. With a sudden flash of resourceful inspiration, you snatch the picture from its hook and bring it down on top of one of the wasp-like horrors.

You let go of the canvas and the painting falls to the floor, trapping the critter beneath it. With barely a thought you take a step forward and stamp down hard on the back of the picture with both feet. You are rewarded with the wet crunch of the creature being crushed beneath it.

But there is still your second adversary to deal with. As the next angry bug comes at you, you grab hold of a heavy velvet drape and swing it at the creature. As the fabric billows open, it catches the insect within it. And then, as it comes back to you, it does so with the wasp-beetle trapped within the folds of cloth.

Not waiting to see how long it takes the insect to escape from its confinement, you bound down the hall and, with still no other human presence making itself felt, fling open the front door and run out into the chill night.

Take **+1 COMBAT** and turn to **264**.

246

You have had enough of this place. The morgue unnerves you deeply and you can't stay here a moment longer.

If you have picked up a [TOE-TAG], turn to **286**.
If not, turn to **266**.

You remain alone, or so it would seem, within the mysterious mansion.

Where do you want to look now in the hunt for answers?

If you want to explore the west wing of the house, turn to **176**.

If you want to try the double doors to your right, turn to **267**.

"Professor Nidus's rooms are on the second floor, beyond the Kafka collection," Dr Christopher tells you. "Actually, tell you what, let me show you."

Take the SECRET: *The Entomologist.*

The entomologist accompanies you out of his office, before pulling the door to and locking it. He then leads you through the Science Building, upstairs and along corridors, until he comes to a halt before a dark walnut door, next to which is a brass plaque bearing the professor's name.

"I'm not sure she'll still be here at this late hour," he says, tapping on the door. He turns the handle, and the door opens a crack. "Professor Nidus?" Dr Christopher asks as he steps over the threshold.

The room beyond is in darkness but an angry buzzing sound immediately alerts you to the danger you are in. Senses straining, peering intently at the gloom, in the hope that it might reveal its secrets, you follow the sound as it draws nearer. The room is suddenly bathed in light as Dr Christopher finds a light switch and the scientist cries out in wordless horror as the danger that threatens the two of you is thrown into stark relief.

It has the appearance of a colossal hornet, a foot in length and with a wingspan twice that. Your eyes move from the monstrous insect's snapping mandibles to the glistening stinger hanging from its bulbous abdomen. Grabbing the closest thing you can find to a weapon, you prepare for the inevitable, as the demonic wasp glides toward you on its blurring wings.

You may spend **1 RESOURCES** at the start of each round to add 2 to your total for that round.

Round one: roll two dice and add your **COMBAT**. If you have the Weakness {**FEAR OF INSECTS**} deduct 2. If the total is 12 or more, you win the first round.

Round two: roll two dice and add your **COMBAT**. If you have the Weakness {**FEAR OF INSECTS**} deduct 2. If you won the first round, add 2. If your total is 13 or more, you win the second round.

> If you won the second round, turn to **288**.
> If you lost the second round, turn to **268**.

As you prepare to deal with those that remain, reality itself begins to buckle. The walls of the conservatory ripple, as if you are perceiving them as a reflection in a pool of water, but then the ripple is drawn into a vortex of spiraling light and matter. A howling wind fills the building, like a hurricane sucking all into it – bulbous insects, uprooted plants, screaming cultists, et al – as the geometries of the house start to collapse, the walls folding in on themselves in an insane, infinite, origami loop.

Reality itself cannot endure the warping effects of two rents in the veil of spacetime being so close to one another. Trapped within Abaddan House, you do not escape its ultimate fate. The only comfort is that you are gone long before the building makes the translation to the uncaring cosmos of another dimension.

The End.

Despite the taxing travails you have suffered this night, much needed adrenaline gives your body the kick it needs, and you flee from Abaddan House, the cries of the battling cultists and the droning voice of the swarm fading into the distance. But as you retrace the route you took to get here and find yourself outside, swaddled by the cold night air once more, something unbelievable and world-warping occurs.

You feel tremors under your feet and a sudden drop in air pressure, all of which is accompanied by the howling of a hurricane. You continue to flee through the grounds. Risking no more than a glance over your shoulder, you witness what is happening to the house. The mansion appears to be collapsing. Impossible geometries take hold of the building as it begins to fold in on itself, brick walls bending, pitched roofs buckling, and windows shattering in their frames, as those same apertures are crushed shut.

You do not stop running, but increase your effort, panic driving you to exhaustion. Moonlight chases you as the eclipse passes and you look to the sky to see the moon has returned, the hole in the sky and the entity that lurked beyond it, both having vanished. Fatigued, your legs and lungs burning, you stumble to a halt and gaze across the moonlit estate. But of Abaddan House there is no sign. There is not even a footprint on the ground where it previously stood, no sign of a basement or wine cellar. Nothing at all but a sweep of untouched turf. It is as if the house never existed at all. In fact, your memories of the place are already starting to evaporate.

But what of Dr Blaine? What happened to him? The evidence, or lack of it, would suggest that the warring cults have, if not actually obliterated each other, nonetheless caused each other a major setback. But Dr Blaine had nothing to do with either the Swarm God or Silenus. Has he been transported to wherever it is that Abaddan House has gone, or did his patron deity see fit to save him at the end? Perhaps he used his god given powers to transport himself to safety at the final moment?

But the answers to such questions will have to wait until after you have had something to eat and drink. As you set off for Velma's Diner once more, tendrils of black cloud arch across the heavens and you can't shake the feeling that by setting the Outer Gods against each other, the dread prophecy has been fulfilled regardless.

Take the SECRET: *The Haunter in the Dark.*

Final score: 3 stars.

The End.

"It almost doesn't look like a language so much as a code," you say.

"Very good," says your guide to the esoteric. "It is an ancient language. Entire epochs have come and gone since it was first spoken, and its name is unpronounceable to the uninitiated. But the keeper of this notebook has used the letterforms as the basis for a cypher, rather than writing in the language itself. The trouble is, without the key to the code, whatever is written within will remain as it appears now – unintelligible."

A key? Turning back to the flyleaf, where Dr Blaine had written where to return the notebook, if found, you focus on the curious symbols written faintly in pencil underneath. You must have only registered them subconsciously before but register them you did. Could this be the key to unlocking the code?

Property of Dr Blaine, Zoology Department,
School of Life Sciences, Miskatonic University.

Turning back to the page Miriam Beecher was showing you, you flick between the two, Miriam exhorting your efforts as you try to discern meaning from the seemingly meaningless.

Can you decode [DR BLAINE'S NOTEBOOK]? If so,
can you see the secret hidden in plain sight?

If you want to spend **1 CLUE** to help you crack the
code, turn to **285**.
If not, turn to **271**.

252

So, it turns out there are not two factions at play here, who would each see their god ascend this night, but *three*, and you have been helping one of them all along!

A little knowledge is most definitely a dangerous thing, and knowing what you do eats away at the already frayed edges of your mind. After all, if you are directly helping a mad god tighten its already pernicious grip on the world, then what hope is there for Arkham, Massachusetts?

> Lose - **1 SANITY** and turn to **181**.

253

Everyone else present within the conservatory might have lost their minds – including Dr Blaine – but you are determined not to go the same way. You are here to fight the madness and prevent it from consuming the world! Take **+1 WILLPOWER**.

Tearing your gaze from the woman's eyes, you focus instead on your hands and the means you have at your disposal to deal the Cult of the Empty Sky a fatal blow, and strike your attacker, sending her reeling.

> Turn to **181**.

It's no good. In the heat of the moment, you cannot think of a way to use the alcohol to set fire to the insects quickly enough and, before you know it, you are having to resort to other measures. In your panic to defend yourself, you fumble the items you are holding and manage to drop them both on the floor, where the bottle of alcohol breaks.

Strike the [LIGHTER] and the [WHISKEY] or the [SWABBING ALCOHOL] from your Character Sheet and turn to **220**.

Cautiously, with arms and legs shaking, you make your way back to the projecting dormer and use that to assist your descent of the angled roof tiles until you can climb over the windowsill and back into the office.

And there waiting for you are four burly police officers, red in the face and panting for breath, having run up two flights stairs to Dr Blaine's study. Behind them, in the doorway, stands a jittery-looking secretary.

"Hands in the air!" the sergeant leading them shouts, and you do as he says as the other policemen train their guns on you.

Turn to **262**.

Doing nothing to disrupt the ritual, you watch and wait.

The incomprehensible chanting becomes infused with an intense buzzing as the cultists repeat the name of their god over and over: "Ezel-zen-rezl. Ezel-zen-rezl! *Ezel-zen-rezl!*"

Only the buzzing sound isn't just being made by the ecstatic devotees of the swarm, it is being produced by the buzzing insects that fill the conservatory too. And by something else. As you continue to watch and wait, the ritual reaches its climax, the voices of the cult raised in jubilation. Professor Nidus throws her hands into the air and from the mouth of the clay pot pours a torrent of huge black insects. They look like a grotesque cross between a scarab beetle and a tarantula hawk. The creatures quickly fill the conservatory, blackening the air and blocking your view of what is happening upon the plinth. In mere moments hundreds have emerged from the impossible vessel, then thousands, then tens of thousands. Then the screaming begins.

Dr Blaine has mistimed things terribly. You hear him give voice to an exclamation of bitter regret before his words are drowned out by the buzzing voice of the swarm.

Ezel-zen-rezl is not one being but a gestalt entity, an incomprehensibly huge hive mind made up of billions of the creatures the Cult of Assimilation calls trylogogs. A portion of this impossible swarm emerges now, using the cicada vessel as a way into the world, like some Biblical plague of locusts. And like locusts, the trylogogs start to scour the conservatory of all organic matter, intending to ultimately make it part of Ezel-zen-rezl. That includes all the exotic plants growing in the conservatory, every single one of the cultists trapped within, Professor Nidus, Dr Blaine...

And you.

The End.

There are just too many of them and the two of you are overwhelmed by sheer force of numbers. The tables turned, you are taken captive by the cultists. You struggle against the iron hold of the twisted men and women but there are too many of them and, in the end, you must admit that you aren't going anywhere. It would appear that all is lost.

> Make a fate test. Roll one die, and if you have the Weakness {CURSED} add 1. If the result is equal to or lower than the current **DOOM** level, turn to **232**.
>
> If not, turn to **177**.

You manage to tear your eyes away from the emerging monstrosity at last, although it takes a physical toll to do so. But your focus on the hole in the sky has been noticed by Silenus's servant, the mysterious Dr Waugh. At a shout from the leader the Cult of the Empty Sky, beating its smoke-like wings, his monstrous steed takes off from where it is perched at the edge of the shattered conservatory roof and swoops down into the space. Clearly, he intends to do away with you, probably for daring to cast your eyes upon his unholy master. You have no choice but to prepare yourself for battle.

This is going to be a tough fight. You may spend **1 RESOURCES** at the start of each round to add 2 to your total for that round.

Round one: roll two dice and add your **COMBAT** and your **WILLPOWER**, but then deduct the current **DOOM** level. If you have the {SECRET RITES} Ability, add 1. If the total is 18 or more, you win the first round.

Round two: roll two dice and add your **COMBAT** and your **WILLPOWER**. If you have the {SECRET RITES} Ability, add 1. If you won the first round, add 2. If your total is 19 or more, you win the second round.

Round three: roll two dice and add your **COMBAT** and your **WILLPOWER**. If you have the {SECRET RITES} Ability, add 1. If you won the second round, add 2. If your total is 20 or more, you win the third round.

If you won the third round, turn to **146**.
If you lost the third round, turn to **284**.

259

Your investigation appears to have hit a dead end. With no idea what to do next you have no choice but to go home. But as you walk the dark streets of Arkham alone, you cannot shake the feeling of impending doom that has settled over you.

Take the SECRET: *Dead End*.

The End.

260

Faced with such insanity, what sane response is there other than to flee? But between you and freedom stand battling cultists, swarming insects, and several closed doors.

It's time for an escape minigame. Roll one die and add 1 if you have the {AGILE} Ability.

> If the total is equal to or less than your **HEALTH**, turn to **100**.
>
> If the total is greater than your **HEALTH**, turn to **26**.

Detective Harden listens intently as you share with him what you have learned. He raises his eyebrows at some of what you tell him, but never challenges you regarding its veracity.

"I'm not in the habit of doing this sort of thing," he says when you have finished, "but I can't have you out there not able to look after yourself. Here" – he reaches into a coat pocket and takes out a [FLICK KNIFE], which he slips to you across the table – "take this, and be careful."

Take the SECRET: *To Protect and Serve*.

If you want to take the [FLICK KNIFE], take +1 RESOURCES, and if you have the Weakness {PARANOID}, you do not have it any longer; strike it from your Character Sheet. Detective Harden's attitude has reminded you that not everyone in Arkham is out to get you.

The interview over, you leave the Police Station with the intention of looking elsewhere.

Spend either 1 CLUE or 1 RESOURCES, or take +1 DOOM, and then turn to 140.

Before you know it, the gruff sergeant is informing you of your supposed crimes, while his rookie colleague goes to handcuff you. You are the chief suspect in what has suddenly become the homicide of Dr Blaine of Miskatonic University's Life Sciences Department.

> If you want to go quietly, turn to **282**.
> If you would rather resist arrest, turn to **299**.

Pulling the box out from under the desk, you open it and find that it is lined with velvet that is a deep blue in color. Lying snuggled within the velvet is an ornate **[BRASS TELESCOPE]**. It is a far more primitive device than that which the budding astronomers studying at the university use to observe the heavens, but it is also far more beautiful.

If you want to take the **[BRASS TELESCOPE]** with you, record it on your Character Sheet and take **+1 RESOURCES**.

> Take the SECRET: *Spyglass* and turn to **14**.

Needing some time to think, and somewhere you can go where you won't be looking over your shoulder the whole time in fear of something coming for you out of the darkness, you walk the streets of Arkham until you find yourself outside Velma's Diner once more.

Entering, you take a seat at an empty corner booth lit by a warm yellow lamp. The eatery is quiet at this time of night, but not entirely empty, and it is not long before a steaming mug of bitter coffee and a piece of cake is placed in front of you. Both are most welcome. Take +1 **HEALTH** and +1 **WILLPOWER**.

The more of this mystery you uncover, the more you realize that you must better prepare yourself in order to fight the coming darkness. Lost in thought, as you consider all that has happened to you since you last enjoyed the security of the diner – even though you didn't appreciate it at the time – all that you have witnessed, and the curious artifacts you have discovered, you do not notice the presence of the other until he takes a seat opposite you.

Looking up at the waistcoat-wearing, gray-bearded gentleman, you strangle a cry of surprise so that it escapes your lips as nothing more than a breathless gasp. From behind wire-rimmed spectacles, the man fixes you with eyes that twinkle like the stars in the night sky. Finding your voice again you manage to stammer the words, "Dr Blaine, I presume."

If you have a [HANDKERCHIEF], turn to **244**.
If not, but you have [DETECTIVE HARDEN'S CARD], turn to **198**.
If not, but you have [INKY FINGERS], turn to **230**.
If not, but you have [WET SHOES], turn to **209**.
If you have none of these things, turn to **182**.

Perhaps the Orne Library contains documents relating to Professor Nidus's family home. Deduct - **1 CLUE**.

If you know the name of the house where the Professor lives, turn the letters of the two-word name into numbers, using the code A=1, B=2... Z=26, add them up, multiply the result by two, and then turn to the same section as the total.

If the section you turn to makes no sense you will have to leave the library and look elsewhere for clues: turn to **140**.

You push open the door and hurry back through the hospital building, eager to get out of there as quickly as possible.

It feels like there are powers at work behind the scenes, moving their pawns into position, as if they are preparing for war, or the fulfilment of some prophecy. And [DR BLAINE'S NOTEBOOK] is what got you caught up in this mystery in the first place. Perhaps there is something in there that could help you now. Or perhaps there is some message you have received that could grant you much needed insight.

If there is, you will have four numbers associated with this piece of information. Add them together and turn to the section that has the same number as the total.

> If you don't know of anything that could help you, turn to **259**.

267

As you creep toward the doors, the faint susurrus becomes incrementally louder, but you cannot determine whether it is an insect-like buzzing you can hear or the whispering of dozens of human voices.

> If you want to open the door, turn to **151**.
> If you want to put your ear to the door and listen for a moment or two before opening it, turn to **287**.

268

The hideous creature dodges your flailing defense and, swinging its tail underneath it, manages to jab you with its lethal sting. The shock of the puncture wound causes you to cry out but then the real pain hits, and all the sound is stolen from your lungs as you double-up in agony. It feels as if your flesh is on fire, spreading from the spot where the barbed tip has pierced your skin. Lose - **1 HEALTH**.

As you crumple, your eyes screwed up tight, unable to do anything other than try to breathe through the pain and gritted teeth, you hear a crash – as of something heavy hitting a table – accompanied by a shout from your companion.

"Take that, you fiend!" Dr Christopher cries.

As the initial shock of the injury you have sustained begins to pass, you open your eyes again. Through tears of pain, you see the entomologist, a patrician stone head raised in one hand, panting in shock himself as he stares at the grotesque creature he has crushed against a desk using the heavy marble bust.

"Have you ever seen anything like that before?" you ask as you recover your breath.

"I'm afraid I have," Dr Christopher replies, his face grim.

As befits a professor of entomology, Professor Nidus's office is full of vivaria, containing slices of various global habitats, from sandy deserts to misty rainforests. Under the glow of the electric light, the room's occupants have come to skittering, scurrying life. Behind the glass of the sampled ecosystems are thousands upon thousands of insects – everything from hissing cockroaches, mantises and soldier ants, to various lepidoptera, locusts, and killer wasps.

Did the professor know about the giant hornet in her office? Could there be a nest of these horrors somewhere nearby? Is she in danger? Or did she put it here?

There is a photograph prominently displayed on one wall of the office. It shows a grand, colonial style mansion, set within its own wooded estate. Standing in front of the house is a man dressed in tweed, and his wife, and between them a serious-looking girl of no more than seven years, sporting a severe bob. Etched into the negative so that it appears in white letters on the developed photograph is the name of the place: *Abaddan House*. Take the SECRET: *Family Photo*.

"That's Professor Nidus's ancestral home," Dr Christopher says, seeing you examining the photo. "That's probably where she is right now."

Thanking him for his help, you decide it's time to take your search for answers elsewhere.

Take + **1 CLUE** and turn to **140**.

You and your companion have battled your way past the first wave of cultists – take **+1 COMBAT** – but you are not out of danger yet.

You have the cultists on the backfoot now. But where one falls, like the many-headed Hydra of classical mythology, where one falls there always seems to be two to take their place. After all, the entire Arkham branch of the Cult of Assimilation is here to see their god brought into the world and be made one with Ezel-zen-rezl.

So, what do you want to do?

> Continue to fight your way through the cultists to reach Professor Nidus: turn to **294**.
>
> Look for something you can use against the devotees of the Lord of Swarms (if you haven't already): turn to **48**.

You suddenly find yourself surrounded by a horde of hideous insects. You get the impression of hornet-like bodies, bulging multi-faceted eyes, bristly black carapaces, whirring wings, large mandibles, and cruelly barbed stingers. The relentless droning of the critters fills your skull. You can feel them crawling all over you – in your hair, over your eyes – and stifle a cry of revulsion, in case, were you to open your mouth, some of them might actually get inside.

How can you fight a swarm of insects? You're about to find out. You may spend **1 RESOURCES** at the start of each round to add 2 to your total for that round.

Round one: roll two dice and add your **COMBAT** and your **INTELLECT**. If the total is 10 or more, you win the first round.

Round two: roll two dice and add your **COMBAT** and your **INTELLECT**. If you won the first round, add 2. If your total is 11 or more, you win the second round.

> If you won the second round, turn to **290**.
> If you lost the second round, turn to **274**.

"I have an idea," the proprietor of Ye Olde Magick Shoppe says, a guileless expression on her face. "Leave the notebook with me and I'll see if I can decode it for you. What do you say?"

How do you feel about handing [DR BLAINE'S NOTEBOOK] over to Miriam Beecher?

> If you want to go along with her suggestion, turn to **291**.
> If you don't want to give her [DR BLAINE'S NOTEBOOK], turn to **141**.

You attempt to fight your way through the swarm as best you can but there are simply too many insects to overcome. In spite of the fact that you are fighting it as if it were one creature it is, of course, composed of thousands of individuals, meaning that the swarm can effectively avoid injury or replace destroyed parts of itself with ease.

Struggling to the foot of the dais, you see Professor Nidus standing atop it with her hands outstretched in triumph and realize that she has done what was needed to complete the ritual.

In the next instant, a torrent of huge black insects pours from the mouth of the curious clay pot. They look like some grotesque amalgamation of a scarab beetle and a tarantula hawk. Their presence blackens the air around you and blocks your view of what is happening upon the dais. In mere moments hundreds of the horrors have emerged from the impossible vessel, then thousands, then tens of thousands. By then the screaming has already begun.

It takes a moment for you to realize that it is you who is screaming, as the locust-like insects devour everything within the conservatory, so that it might be assimilated into the hive of Ezel-zen-rezl.

Take the SECRET: *Ezel-zen-rezl Rising.*

The End.

Opening the bottle, you take a swig of the alcohol but hold it in your mouth. Flicking the lighter open, you thumb the flint and a warm orange flame pops into being around the exposed wick. Holding the lighter out before you, you send a mist of highly flammable alcohol spraying from your mouth, over the flame, and into the path of the swarm. Your improvised flamethrower causes several of the insects to instantly catch light and fall out of the air. The others buzz angrily and fly up toward the ceiling, out of harm's way. You repeat the action, and more of the disgusting bugs drop to the tiled floor as little more than blackened crispy husks. But before you can spray them again, the lighter's flame dies; its fuel reservoir must have been almost empty to begin with.

Having held the swarm at bay, you back toward the door to the morgue, throwing the remainder of the bottle of alcohol into the room, and make your escape from the hospital. Strike the [LIGHTER] and the [SWABBING ALCOHOL] or [WHISKEY] from your Character Sheet and take +1 INTELLECT.

It feels like there are powers at work behind the scenes, moving their pawns into position, as if they are preparing for war, or the fulfilment of some prophecy. And [DR BLAINE'S NOTEBOOK] is what got you caught up in this mystery in the first place. Perhaps there is something in there that could help you now. Or perhaps there is some message you have received that could grant you much needed insight.

If there is, you will have four numbers associated with this piece of information. Add them together and turn to the section that has the same number as the total.

> If you don't know of anything that could help you, turn to **259**.

274

You bat at the bulbous insect bodies with your hands, unable to suppress your mewling cries of revulsion, but it is like trying to fight the wind. No matter what you do, you cannot escape the droning horde. Steadily backing toward the only exit from the morgue, in the end you give up trying the fight the swarm and turn tail and flee, bursting through the door, which is inexplicably no longer barred shut. But as you are running back down the corridor from the nurse's station, before you can escape the hospital, several of the monstrous insects make good use of their snapping mandibles and glistening stingers. Lose -**2 HEALTH**.

It feels like there are powers at work behind the scenes, moving their pawns into position, as if they are preparing for war, or the fulfilment of some prophecy. And [DR BLAINE'S NOTEBOOK] is what got you caught up in this mystery in the first place. Perhaps there is something in there that could help you now. Or perhaps there is some message you have received that could grant you much needed insight.

If there is, you will have four numbers associated with this piece of information. Add them together and turn to the section that has the same number as the total.

> If you don't know of anything that could help you, turn to **259**.

Having dithered here, you can see no other option available to you now other than to bring the fight to the cultists. You may spend **1 RESOURCES** at the start of each round to add 2 to your total for that round.

Round one: roll two dice and add your **COMBAT**, but then deduct the current **DOOM** level. If you have the {**AGILE**} Ability, add 1. If the total is 17 or more, you win the first round.

Round two: roll two dice and add your **COMBAT**. If you have the {**AGILE**} Ability, add 1. If you won the first round, add 2. If your total is 18 or more, you win the second round.

> If you won the second round, turn to **269**.
> If you lost the second round, turn to **257**.

Things are starting to settle down again now since the grim discovery was made in Dr Blaine's office. Most of the police vehicles have left, and while a few groups of students remain, huddled together against the cold, speculating on what might have happened to the zoology lecturer, most have sensibly decided to retreat to their rooms for the night and lock their doors behind them. Take the SECRET: *Location Three.*

You won't have a hope of getting to Dr Blaine's study now without arousing the suspicions of the authorities and, since it has been designated a scene of investigation, it is being watched full-time by armed police officers.

If you want to search for answers here, you are going to need to focus your attentions by choosing a specific place to look, such as the Warren Observatory or the Orne Library.

Take **+ 2 DOOM** and turn to **140** to try another, specific location. You may spend **1 CLUE** or **1 RESOURCES** to reduce the **DOOM** penalty by 1; spend **2 CLUES** or **2 RESOURCES** to avoid adding any **DOOM**.

277

Back in the study, you consider the jumbled collection of books, papers, and the stuffed animals in glass cases. There are three places that are most likely to furnish you with the answers you are so desperately seeking: Dr Blaine's desk; a large pinboard, adorned with all manner of bits of paper; and the large bookcase that covers the entirety of the wall opposite.

To study the pinboard (if you haven't done so already), turn to **195**.

To examine the large bookcase (if you haven't done so already), turn to **175**.

To search the desk (if you haven't done so already), turn to **154**.

To leave the room without further delay, turn to **215**.

278

The madness that has possessed the followers of Silenus is infectious. What is the point in going on, you think, when all that awaits the cosmos is heat death and the end of all life, anyway? Lose - **1 SANITY**.

In that moment, the woman strikes you, causing you a savage wound. Lose - **1 HEALTH.**

However, her attack also knocks some sense back into you and you dispel such negative thoughts from your mind while delivering your attacker a blow that sends her reeling.

Turn to **181.**

The gothic structure that is St Mary's Hospital looms over the surrounding tenements and brownstones of Uptown, a shadowy architectural mass that appears black against the purpling sky. Windows across all six stories of the structure spill light into the darkness but just as many remain in darkness.

No matter the time of day or night, being the only hospital in Arkham, there always seems to be a steady stream of people visiting the receiving room. You join a mother accompanying a child with a bucket stuck on its head and a young man walking with the aid of a pair of crutches as they enter the imposing edifice, but accidentally step in a dirty puddle that has collected in a pothole. Record your **[WET SHOES]** on your Character Sheet.

Once inside, you follow signs to the only place Dr Blaine's body could have been taken: the morgue.

Passing through a door beside a nurse's station, you

descend a flight of stairs to the basement level of the hospital. Through another door you eventually find the entrance to the morgue itself. However, hearing the squeak of a wheel bearing in need of oil, you catch sight of a nurse pushing a gurney along the poorly lit passageway, heading away from you.

> If you want to call out to ask for help, turn to **4**.
> If you want to go about your business without drawing attention to yourself, turn to **36**.

280

The dread power that emanates from the levitating sorcerer is a palpable presence. Not only are you unable to challenge his supremacy, your tenuous hold on what is left of your sanity is threatening to give up and unravel in the face of such mind-bending power as well.

Roll one die, and if you have either or both the {CURSED} or {HAUNTED} Weaknesses, deduct 1.

> If the total is equal to or less than your **SANITY**, turn to **260**.
> If the total is greater than your **SANITY**, turn to **206**.

You came here to stop Professor Nidus, and by extension the Cult of Assimilation, and that is what you intend to do. Any other concerns are secondary and will have to wait until your primary mission is complete – and that means joining those who have sworn themselves to Silenus in attacking the followers of the Swarm God. You may spend 1 **RESOURCES** at the start of each round to add 2 to your total for that round.

Round one: roll two dice and add your **COMBAT**, but then deduct the current **DOOM** level. If you have the {AGILE} Ability, add 1. If the total is 16 or more, you win the first round.

Round two: roll two dice and add your **COMBAT**. If you have the {AGILE} Ability, add 1. If you won the first round, add 2. If your total is 16 or more, you win the second round.

If you won the second round, turn to **181**.
If you lost the second round, turn to **92**.

There is little point trying to escape when the policealready have you in their clutches, not to mention the fact that there are four of them. There will be time to resolve this misunderstanding later. After all, you need to take charge for you are all too aware of how vital information related to certain investigations can go missing on an all too regular basis. And so, for now, you allow yourself to be led away and bundled into one of the cars, which then carries you across town to the Police Station in Easttown.

> Take the Weakness {CRIMINAL} and turn to 59.

283

You let the door swing open wide and search for a light switch, not entering the room until it is bathed in bright white light.

Befitting of a professor of entomology, as well as the expected desk and bookshelves, the room is full of vivaria, containing slices of various global habitats, from sandy deserts to misty rainforests. Under the glow of the electric lights, the room's occupants have come to skittering, scurrying life. Behind the glass of the captured ecosystems are thousands upon thousands of insects – hissing cockroaches, mantises, soldier ants, butterflies, moths, locusts, and killer wasps.

Professor Nidus clearly isn't here, and you don't have any strong desire to linger here any longer than is necessary – the presence of the myriad insects is making your skin crawl – but you do notice two things that you decide deserve closer scrutiny before you leave.

One is a photograph of a grand, colonial style mansion, set within its own wooded estate. Standing in front of the house is a man dressed in tweed, and his wife, and between them a serious-looking girl of no more than seven years, sporting a severe bob. Etched into the negative so that it appears in white letters on the developed photograph is the name of the place: *Abaddan House*. Take the SECRET: *Family Photo*.

The other is a curious, and rather morbid mask, made from a human skull. If you want to take the [SKULL MASK] with you, record it on your Character Sheet and take +1 RESOURCES.

Turn to **140**.

The creature's toothed beak seems all too corporeal when the monster catches you up in its jaws and tosses your limp body into the air, before catching it again and swallowing you whole. Whatever happens next, you are not conscious to witness it.

The End.

You realize that the symbols written under Dr Blaine's note on the flyleaf are the key to cracking the code: each one relates to the letter in the same place in the message written in English. Deduct -1 CLUE.

Having decoded the rest of the text, you will see that some of them are numbers. Could they help you work out where to turn next?

If not, turn to **271**.

You put your hand to the door and push. It gives only a little before meeting resistance. You push harder, but the doors will not open. Taking hold of the handle you rattle the doors violently, but it will not budge. You are trapped!

As you are wondering what could be preventing the doors from opening, a buzzing sound behind you causes you to turn round. The noise is coming from the bank of stainless steel hatches. As you stare in horror, one of the doors creaks open, under the force of whatever is pushing from behind it, and a swarm of black-bodied insects pours into the room through the crack. The tiled walls echo with the angry buzzing of the bugs.

If you want to try forcing the morgue door to open, turn to **8**.
If you want to prepare to defend yourself from the swarm, turn to **270**.

Warily, you lean in close and press your ear to the warm wood. Over the thudding of your own pulse, closing your eyes to help you focus, you listen intently to the sounds being transmitted through the polished mahogany.

It is definitely chanting voices you can hear, but you cannot tell how many. As you listen, you become lulled by the wave-like susurrus of the sound. The overlapping utterances remind you of the surf breaking on the shore. But then, as you listen harder, the lilting voices acquire a buzzing edge that unsettles you and reminds you of the roar of a wasps' nest.

The buzzing becomes louder until it feels like the wasps are inside your skull! The world around you melts away, and in your mind's eye you find yourself atop a hill gazing down at the streets of Arkham. The sun is high in the sky but is almost blotted out by the swarm of monstrous insects that is descending upon the town and you can hear the screams of the townsfolk as they are assimilated by the droning horde. Lose - **1 SANITY.**

Turn to **151.**

The hideous thing attempts to stab you with its elongated stinger, but you manage to dodge or deflect its every attack. And then, at long last, you have the advantage. You manage to strike the wasp and send it crashing to the floor of the office. Before it can recover itself, you slide a pile of books off the edge of a desk and a half-dozen heavy volumes land on top of the horror, crushing its thorax and abdomen.

The wasp thing twitches for a moment and then is still. You have succeeded in killing it! Take **+1 COMBAT.**

A slow handclap, strangely loud in the confines of the office, shakes you out of your stunned reverie and Dr Christopher says, "Well done. Well done indeed! I only hope you have left enough for me to examine back at my office."

"Have you ever seen anything like that before?" you ask as you recover your breath.

"I'm afraid I have," Dr Christopher replies, his face grim.

As befits a professor of entomology, Professor Nidus's office is full of vivaria, containing slices of various global habitats, from sandy deserts to misty rainforests. Under the glow of the electric light, the room's occupants have come to skittering, scurrying life. Behind the glass of the sampled ecosystems are thousands upon thousands of insects – everything from hissing cockroaches, mantises and soldier ants, to various lepidoptera, locusts, and killer wasps.

Did the professor know about the giant hornet in her office? Could there be a nest of these horrors somewhere nearby? Is she in danger? Or did she put it here?

You notice two other things of note within the room that have nothing to do with insects but deserve closer scrutiny, nonetheless. The first is a curious, and rather morbid, human [SKULL MASK]. If you want to take it with you, record it on your Character Sheet and take +1 RESOURCES.

The second is a photograph of a grand, colonial style mansion, set within its own wooded estate. Standing in front of the house is a man dressed in tweed, and his wife, and between them a serious looking girl of no more than seven years, sporting a severe bob. Etched into the negative so that it appears in white letters on the developed photograph is the name of the place: *Abaddan House.* Take the SECRET: *Family Photo.*

"That's Professor Nidus's ancestral home," Dr Christopher says, seeing you examining the photo. "That's probably where she is right now."

Thanking him for his help, you decide it's time to take your search for answers elsewhere.

Take +2 CLUES and turn to 140.

288

289

As if already fully aware of what you are intending, Dr Blaine turns his head to regard you, trapping you within the burning gaze of his pupilless eyes.

"Sniveling worm," he spits. "You dare to challenge me? You have served your purpose but now you are expendable. Your services are no longer required."

He points at you and one of the writhing tendrils of shadow reaches toward you, rippling its way across the wall, and then, somehow, you are caught in its grasp. You feel something cold and muscular wrap about your body and start to squeeze. There is nothing you can do as the sorcerer's shadow-limb constricts, pulling tighter. As it does so, bones break until you mercifully lose consciousness.

The End.

290

You grab what's to hand, sending a pile of scalpels and other sterilized tools clattering to the floor, and proceed to swat at the bulbous insects with the enameled piece of metal you now have grasped in both hands. Buzzing things are sent tumbling to the floor, their wings broken, while others are splatted between the tray and the wall, or the tray and the trolleys. Eventually, those that remain leave you alone and alight on the shrouded corpses or bump against the shaded lamps that bathe the morgue in a jaundiced yellow light. Take +1 COMBAT.

Turning your attention to the door once more, you rattle the handles until gravity causes the broom, or whatever it is that has been jammed through them, to slide free, enabling you to make your escape at last. You cannot bear to remain in St Mary's Hospital a moment longer and run from the place as fast as your feet will carry you.

It feels like there are powers at work behind the scenes, moving their pawns into position, as if they are preparing for war, or the fulfilment of some prophecy. And [DR BLAINE'S NOTEBOOK] is what got you caught up in this mystery in the first place. Perhaps there is something in there that could help you now. Or perhaps there is some message you have received that could grant you much needed insight.

If there is, you will have four numbers associated with this piece of information. Add them together and turn to the section that has the same number as the total.

> If you don't know of anything that could help you, turn to **259**.

You hand Miriam Beecher the jotter. Strike [DR BLAINE'S NOTEBOOK] from your Character Sheet and take -1 RESOURCES and -1 CLUE.

Miriam Beecher tells you to come back tomorrow and with that, ushers you out of the shop.

Take the SECRET: *Hocus Pocus* and turn to **141**.

What is going on? Has the whole world run to madness? Are you the only sane person left within it? You cannot let the arrival of this new faction prevent you from completing your mission. Professor Nidus's ritual must be stopped. Ezel-zen-rezl cannot be permitted to conquer Arkham, and neither can whatever impossible entity Dr Waugh has sold his soul to.

"Members of the Cult of the Empty Sky," Dr Blaine says, as if reading your mind. "They worship Silenus, The Empty Sky. They are nihilists and believe there is no point to anything, and therefore embrace death as the only logical answer. Watch out for them – they fear nothing, least of all their own death."

But perhaps you can work this situation to your own advantage. It would appear the ritual to summon the Swarm God has already been interrupted and the Cult of Assimilation is now focused on ridding the conservatory of Dr Waugh and his followers. If you lent your aid to one of the two warring factions you might resolve this conflict more quickly, one way or another, and then be in a better position to deal with the aftermath. Or you could keep out of things and let the two sides destroy each other, and just hope you're not caught in the crossfire. Then again, you are convinced Dr Blaine knows more about what is going on here than he has deigned to share with you so far.

So, what do you want to do?

> If you want to press home your attack against the followers of the Swarm God, turn to **281**.
> If you want to bring the battle to the worshippers of the Silenus, the Empty Sky, turn to **201**.
> If you want to hold back and demand Dr Blaine tell you the truth, turn to **178**.

293

Many of the buildings are fashioned from mere off-cuts of wood, lacking any details whatsoever. However, others have been shaped to look like the places they represent and have been painted accordingly. You can understand why certain landmarks might have been picked out by the model-maker, but you cannot discern the reasoning behind the inclusion of other peculiar places.

There is the Miskatonic University, complete with a model of the Warren Observatory and the Orne Library. Then there is the Historical Society in Arkham's Southside neighborhood. A less obvious inclusion is Ye Olde Magick Shoppe, in Uptown, and another is a large house in French Hill. Thinking it might be helpful to you later on, you find a piece of paper and a pencil, and make a copy of the town plan and the locations marked upon it.

Add the [TOWN MAP] to your Character Sheet and take +1 CLUE.

Turn to 14.

To take on so many might seem like insanity, but there is nothing sane about the situation you find yourself in now, particularly when you consider the powers that your accomplice is able to bring to bear. You dare not dwell on the question of where he draws such power from.

You may spend 1 RESOURCES at the start of each round to add 2 to your total for that round.

Round one: roll two dice and add your COMBAT. If you have the {AGILE} Ability, add 1. If the total is 14 or more, you win the first round.

Round two: roll two dice and add your **COMBAT**. If you won the first round, add 2. If your total is 15 or more, you win the second round. If you lose the third round, Lose -**1 HEALTH**.

Round three: roll two dice and add your **COMBAT**. If you won the second round, add 1, but if you lost the second round, deduct 1. If your total is 14 or more, you win the second round.

> If you won the third round, turn to **13**.
> If you lost the third round, turn to **106**.

Pushing the blade of the [**BONESAW**] through the slight gap between the door and the jamb, you scrape it across the wood until its teeth grip and then furiously work away at it. Forcing the saw backward and forward, you start to cut through the wooden obstruction.

But as you do, you find yourself surrounded by a horde of hideous insects. You try not to look at them too closely and focus on effecting your escape, but you get the impression of hornet-like bodies, bulging multi-faceted eyes, bristly black carapaces, whirring wings, scissoring mandibles, and iridescent spear-tip stinger. The relentless droning of the swarm fills your head. You feel the creatures crawling about all over you, in your hair, around your mouth, over your eyes, and stifle a cry of revulsion, not daring to open your mouth in case some of the horrid things manage to get inside.

At last, the improvised bar breaks and the two ends of the handle clatter to the floor. But the droning horde is not done with you yet. Even as you burst through the door to the morgue, several of the insects manage to sting you, and you can contain your cries of pain no longer. Take -1 HEALTH, -1 SANITY, and the Weakness {FEAR OF INSECTS}.

You cannot bear to remain in St Mary's Hospital a moment longer and run from this place as quickly as you are able.

It feels like there are powers at work behind the scenes, moving their pawns into position, as if they are preparing for war, or the fulfilment of some prophecy. And [DR BLAINE'S NOTEBOOK] is what got you caught up in this mystery in the first place. Perhaps there is something in there that could help you now. Or perhaps there is some message you have received that could grant you much needed insight.

If there is, you will have four numbers associated with this piece of information. Add them together and turn to the section that has the same number as the total.

If you don't know of anything that could help you, turn to **259**.

You consider all the strange objects and arcane artifacts you have discovered since you set out to find the owner of the notebook earlier in the evening. It may only have been a matter of hours ago, but it feels more like a whole week has passed, you have been party to so many strange occurrences since then.

What do you have in your possession that you think might have power over Dr Blaine?

To use the {SORCERY} Ability (if you can), turn to **229**.
To attack the sorcerer with a [BLACK TALON], if you have one, turn to **163**.
To turn the Blade of Ark'at against him, turn to **105**.

These are your kind of people and so you engage them in conversation.

"What's going on?" you ask.

"Suspected homicide," says Detective Harden, who is in charge here. "Victim is one Dr Blaine."

"Are you looking for anyone in particular in relation to his death?" you ask.

"Not yet," says Harden, "although knowing what these Miskatonic types are like, it was probably another member of his faculty. Dead men's shoes and all that."

At that moment, two morticians emerge from the Science Building, carrying a body on a stretcher between them.

You nod toward the shape of the body beneath the blanket. "Is that the victim?"

"That's him. They're taking him to St Mary's for a full autopsy." The detective pauses, a dark cloud passing over his face as he considers what he's about to say next. "There's something strange about this one."

"You could say that about every other suspicious death in Arkham."

"You're not wrong there," he laughs, handing you a small rectangle of card printed with his name and a telephone number.

"If you hear anything, you can contact me on this number. Someone will take a message if I'm not there."

You thank him and put [DETECTIVE HARDEN'S CARD] in a coat pocket.

If you have a [BLACK TALON], turn to **121**.
If not, turn to **140**.

Making your way through the Science Building, up the stairs and along corridors, you finally find what you are looking for and stop in front of a dark walnut door next to which is a brass plaque bearing the professor's name.

You are about to tap on the door when you decide to try the handle instead. It turns and the door opens a crack. "Professor Nidus?" you call softly, but no reply comes from the darkened room beyond.

> If you want to enter Professor Nidus's office uninvited, turn to **283**.
> If you would prefer to look in on Dr Milan Christopher, if you haven't already, turn to **168**.

You pull away from the young cop and make a break for it, hoping to flee from the police officers before they know what's going on. But this isn't the first time officers of the Arkham Police Department have had to deal with an absconding suspect.

The sergeant sticks out a foot, tripping you and sending you sprawling on the gravel. Lose - **1 HEALTH** because of the painful grazes you suffer to your hands and knees.

Before you can pick yourself up, the cops drag you roughly to your feet, cuff your hands behind your back and bundle you into one of the police cars, which then carries you across town to the Police Station in Easttown.

Take the Weakness {CRIMINAL} and turn to **59**.

300

Despite the taxing travails you have suffered this night, much needed adrenaline gives your body the kick it needs, and you flee from Abaddan House, the cries of the battling cultists and the droning voice of the swarm fading into the distance.

But as you retrace the route you took to get here and find yourself outside, swaddled by the cold night air once more, something unbelievable and world warping occurs. You feel tremors under your feet and a sudden drop in air pressure, all of which is accompanied by the howling of a hurricane. You flee through the grounds.

Risking no more than a glance over your shoulder, you witness what is happening to the house. The mansion appears to be collapsing. Impossible geometries take hold of the building as it begins to fold in on itself, brick walls bending, pitched roofs buckling, and windows shattering in their frames, as those same apertures are crushed shut. You do not stop running, but increase your effort, panic driving you to exhaustion. Moonlight chases you as the eclipse passes and you look to the sky to see the moon has returned, the hole in the sky and the entity that lurked beyond it, both having vanished.

Fatigued, your legs and lungs burning, you stumble to a halt and gaze across the moonlit estate. But of Abaddan House there is no sign. There is not even a footprint on the ground where it previously stood, no sign of a basement or wine cellar. Nothing at all but a sweep of untouched turf. It is as if the house never existed at all. In fact, your memories of the place are already starting to fade.

Does the disappearance of the house indicate the mutual destruction of the rival cults? Or has it come about following the death of the sorcerer of Nyarlathotep, Dr Blaine? At the end of the day, the reason doesn't matter. What is important is the indisputable fact that not only are the mad gods and their worshippers gone, but you have stopped an even more dangerous power rising within Arkham. At least, you hope so.

Suddenly finding yourself in dire need of a cup of coffee and something to eat, you set off for Velma's Diner, where your adventure began, as tentacle-like tendrils of black cloud crawl across the sky above.

Take the SECRET: *The Darkness Over Arkham.*

Final score: 4 stars.

The End.

SECRETS CHECKLIST

As you find these SECRETS in play, check them off the list!

☐ A Curate's Egg
☐ Cracked
☐ Dark Omens
☐ Dead End
☐ Egg Hunter
☐ Ezel-zen-rezl Rising
☐ Family Gallery
☐ Family Photo
☐ Fancy a Bite?
☐ Hunting Nightgaunt
☐ Hocus Pocus
☐ Is This a Dagger I See Before Me?
☐ Live to Fight Another Day
☐ Location One
☐ Location Two
☐ Location Three
☐ Location Four
☐ Location Five
☐ Location Six
☐ Location Seven
☐ Location Eight
☐ Location Nine
☐ Lost in Arkham
☐ Remember, Remember
☐ Hidden One

☐ Hidden Two
☐ Hidden Three
☐ Hidden Four
☐ Hidden Five
☐ Hidden Six
☐ Hidden Seven
☐ Secrets of the Old Ones
☐ Spyglass
☐ The Crawling Chaos
☐ The Darkness Over Arkham
☐ The Detective
☐ The Empty Sky
☐ The Entomologist
☐ The First Casualty
☐ The Fortune-Teller
☐ The Haunter in the Dark
☐ The Historian
☐ The Librarian
☐ The Mortician
☐ To Protect and Serve
☐ War of the Outer Gods
☐ Wisdom of the Ancients
☐ You Can't Make an Omelet Without Breaking Some Eggs

Super-Secrets Checklist

☐ Finish with a combined **COMBAT + INTELLECT + WILLPOWER** of **15** or more: *Hero*.

☐ Finish with at least two stars and a combined **COMBAT + INTELLECT + WILLPOWER** of **5** or less: *On The Brink*.

☐ Finish with 1 or 0 stars: *Ill Met By Moonlight*.

☐ Finish with using three different Investigators: *Defend Arkham At All Costs*.

☐ Finish with *Family Gallery* + *Family Photo*: *Family Album*.

☐ Finish with *Fancy a Bite?* + *Hidden One* + *The Mortician*: *The Darkness Over Arkham*.

☐ Finish with *The Detective* + *The Entomologist* + *The Fortune-Teller* + *The Historian* + *The Librarian*: *Allies*.

☐ Finish the with *A Curate's Egg* + *Cracked* + *Egg Hunter* + *Hidden Three* + *You Can't Make an Omelet Without Breaking Eggs*: *Easter Eggs*.

☐ Finish with a **SANITY** of **5** or more: *Sane*.

☐ Finish with a **HEALTH** of **5** or more: *Fit as a Fiddle*.

☐ Finish with a **DOOM** of **5** or more: *Doomed*.

☐ Finish with **10** or more **CLUES**: *True Detective*.

☐ Finish with **5** or more **RESOURCES**: *Doomsday Prepper*.

☐ Finish with **0 CLUES**: *Lucky*.

☐ Finish with **0 RESOURCES**: *Travelling Light*.

☐ Finish with a **SANITY** of **0** or below, a **HEALTH** of **0** or below, and you collect all **5** weaknesses that can be gained in the game: *Mad, Bad, and Dangerous to Know*.

☐ Finish without cheating even once: *Honesty is the Best Policy*.

☐ Battle 4 different types of monster: *Creature Feature*.

☐ Find the [BONESAW], [BREADKNIFE], [CEREMONIAL DAGGER], [FLICK KNIFE], and [PISTOL] in one playthrough: *Tooled Up*.

☐ Finish with the [BRANDY] and the [WHISKEY]: *Thirsty*.

☐ Finish with [ARCHIBALD'S ACCOUNT], [BLUEPRINT], [DETECTIVE HARDEN'S CARD], [GARDEN PLAN], [DR BLAINE'S NOTEBOOK], and [TOWN MAP]: *Paper Trail*.

☐ Finish with the [CEREMONIAL DAGGER], [CULTISTS ROBES], and [SKULL MASK]: *Caretaker of Ark'at*.

☐ Discover all 24 items across various playthroughs: *Collector*.

☐ Discover all 20 unstarred endings: *Unlucky for Some*.

☐ Discover all 9 Location Secrets: *Location, Location, Location*.

☐ Discover all 7 Secret Secrets: *No Stone Left Unturned*.

☐ Discover all 6 starred endings: *Written in the Stars*.

☐ Collect all 27 Super-Secrets above this one: *Painstaking*.

☐ Collect all 48 in-text Secrets: *Persistent*.

☐ And if you collect both Painstaking and Persistent, award yourself *Obsessed*.

INVESTIGATOR

WILLPOWER	INTELLECT	COMBAT

HEALTH

Loss of Health: If your health falls below 0, you will suffer a penalty equal to it when using your combat value. So, if your health is -1, you must deduct 1 from your combat. If your health is -2, you must deduct 2 from your combat,

SANITY

Loss of Sanity: If your sanity falls below 0, you will suffer a penalty equal to it when using your willpower value. So, if your sanity is -1, you must deduct 1 from your willpower. If your sanity is -2, you must deduct 2 from your intellect, and so on.

RESOURCES	CLUES	DOOM

ITEMS

STARTING ITEM

OTHER ITEMS

ABILITIES

MAJOR ABILITIES

OTHER ABILITIES

WEAKNESSES

MAJOR WEAKNESS

OTHER WEAKNESSES

ACKNOWLEDGMENTS

I have enjoyed my visit to the shadowy streets of Arkham, Massachusetts, immensely. I have a long-held fascination with all things Lovecraftian and have written short stories inspired by the Cthulhu mythos before, but this is the first time I have written a gamebook with such eldritch elements.

I would like to thank the team at Aconyte Books – Marc Gascoigne, Gwendolyn Nix and Matt Keefe – for not only asking me to write this adventure in the first place but helping shape it into what it is now. I would also like to thank the Asmodee Franchise Development Team and Fantasy Flight Games for their guidance and invaluable suggestions. And, lastly, I must thank Victor Cheng for his always thorough and enormously helpful playtesting.

ABOUT THE AUTHOR

JONATHAN GREEN is an award-winning writer of speculative fiction, with more than eighty books to his name. He has written everything from *Fighting Fantasy* gamebooks to *Doctor Who* novels, by way of *Sonic the Hedgehog*, *Star Wars: The Clone Wars*, *Teenage Mutant Ninja Turtles*, and *Judge Dredd*. He is the creator of the *Pax Britannia* steampunk series for Abaddon Books, and the author of the critically-acclaimed, *YOU ARE THE HERO – A History of Fighting Fantasy Gamebooks*. For Aconyte Books, he is the author of *Marvel Multiverse Missions: Moon Knight – Age of Anubis*. He is currently writing his own ACE Gamebooks, which reimagine literary classics as interactive adventures.

ARKHAM HORROR
THE CARD GAME

THE FEAST OF HEMLOCK VALE
INVESTIGATOR & CAMPAIGN
EXPANSION

AVAILABLE NOW!

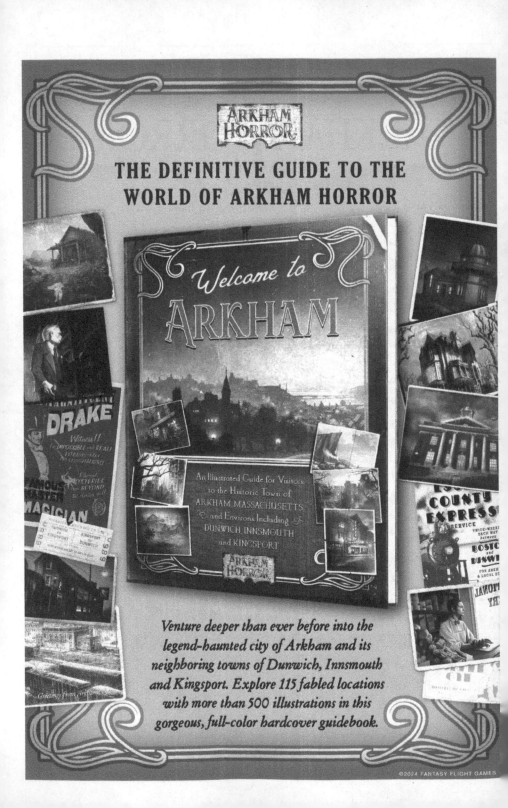

THE DEFINITIVE GUIDE TO THE WORLD OF ARKHAM HORROR

Venture deeper than ever before into the legend-haunted city of Arkham and its neighboring towns of Dunwich, Innsmouth and Kingsport. Explore 115 fabled locations with more than 500 illustrations in this gorgeous, full-color hardcover guidebook.

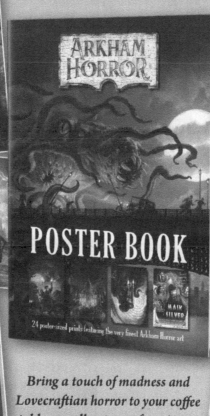